Obscure Pure

M L Pensinger

This book is dedicated to every female reader in hopes of uniting a group of humans who, by all accounts, endure more and are thanked the least. To my Children: Troy, Heather, Shawn, and Tiffany, for their constant love.

Table of Contents

PROLOGUE: May 25th, 1963, 6:00 pm.

The spring weather was as expected in this part of the country, two storm fronts had collided over the area and had stalled. The skies were streaked with bolts of lightning on the horizon, thunder clapped all around, and the wind was sweeping heavy rain across the parking lot of The Lake View General Hospital. Two nurses were waiting inside the double doors for the arrival of the ambulance, the back bottom floor of the hospital was exposed to ground level with a large awing to access emergency vehicles. The ground floor of the hospital was set aside for the operating rooms, lab, morgue, and the county coroner's office.

The back entrance of this world-class hospital afforded the privacy that some very elite patients desired, bringing their team of doctors so they could have cosmetic surgery without publicity. After the necessary nips and tucks were completed, the patients would be transported thirty miles northwest to The Lakewood Sanitarium for a recovery period before reappearing to their public with no one any wiser. Tonight, was different, a patient was arriving from the sanitarium to deliver a baby.

Beth and Mary were two seasoned nurses of the hospital who, for the last several years, had performed administrative work. Beth was the nursing supervisor, and Mary was the head charge nurse. Both nurses were surprised at the assignment when two months prior were summoned to the CEO's office. In the months after the meeting, Beth and Mary would cross paths on hospital related matters and would speculate on the confidentiality of the delivery. Could it be a Hollywood heavyweight who wanted to avoid publicity or a high-ranking government official who had an aide or secretary who, through an illicit affair, resulted in a pregnancy? Whatever the reason, the nurses were sworn to secrecy.

At six O'clock pm, the ambulance arrived from The Lakewood Sanitarium pushing heavy rainwater as it backed under the awning. A gurney was taken out of the ambulance, directed down the hall to operating room number two, and brought to a halt under the massive overhead light.

An unknown man accompanied the patient, and the nurses assumed he was the doctor in charge. Neither Beth nor Mary knew his identity. The doctor never introduced himself or asked the nurses' names, and almost from the start, he seemed arrogant and smug. Over the years, both nurses had worked with many doctors, some more difficult and distant, but both Beth and Mary were shocked by his brash behavior and his insensitivity toward the patient. "Get the patient ready for an internal examination and start an IV" were the first words the doctor spoke, never consulting or consoling the patient or even looking her way. The doctor snapped on a pair of rubber gloves while waiting impatiently for the nurses to carry out his orders with a pure distaste for the procedure on his face. The internal seemed rough, as if the patient were carrying a deadly disease instead of a baby. When he was finished, he removed the gloves, tossed them away and turned to the nurses, asking if there was a doctor's lounge in the area. In a voice that could cut ice, Beth told him to go down the hall and turn right. If the doctor noticed the icy dislike in Beth's voice, he never reacted; instead, he turned on his heels and started heading toward the door. He looked back as if he had forgotten something and gave the following orders, "She is dilated to seven ccs; call me when she is a full nine ccs, or her water has broken."

The nurses turned their attention to the patient; she was under some kind of drugs, her eyes fixed and glassy. She wore the standard cap for surgery, but she also wore a mask to protect her identity. The nurses were able to see the patient was caucasian, medium height, and average weight. She groaned from time to time and was shaking. Mary retrieved an extra blanket, setting the head of the bed in an upward position while mopping the girl's brow. Both nurses felt sorry for the girl. Usually, there were many relatives in the waiting room anxious for news, but this girl only had an uncaring doctor waiting to get the delivery over. Births were to be happy occasions, but this girl was all alone, and that seemed oddly sad.

Beth started the IV as per doctor's orders and started to monitor the vitals of the patient while Mary checked the stats of the fetus. Both nurses agreed it was time for another internal, as it had been one hour and fifteen minutes since the doctor had done his initial examination. The patient had progressed to a full nine ccs, and her labor pains were less than a minute apart. Beth placed a stethoscope on the girl's abdomen and listened, and she was sure she heard two heartbeats. Beth wanted to be sure of her assessment, asking Mary to double check. The results were conclusive: it would be a double delivery, the nurses weren't sure if the doctor possessed this information or even cared.

Mary walked down the hall to retrieve the doctor, informing him of the progress of the patient. Reluctantly, he followed her to the operating room. The doctor went to the scrub area, suited up for the delivery, never inquiring about his patient. He waited for a contraction, and the birth process began. Fifteen minutes later, the first baby was born, it didn't seem to surprise the doctor that the delivery would be twins as he glanced over his mask and announced, "The second baby is a breech."

Breech births weren't uncommon but could be tricky, the doctor ordered the patient be completely sedated, with the IV already in place afforded the sedative to be administered with ease, and the patient was asleep in less than a minute. The baby's buttocks were aimed at the vaginal canal, with its legs sticking straight up in front of the body with the feet near its head. Breech births are more common with multiple births because it is harder for each baby to get into the right position.

The doctor made a cut to prevent tearing, and his quick, precise moves surprised both the nurses. What the doctor lacked in bedside manner, he made up with skill. The clock often became a factor in a breech birth. The doctor slid his hand up the birth canal, relieving the baby's legs. Three minutes had passed, and the clock was ticking. Gently rocking the baby from side to side, the doctor soon realized the baby was lodged, and the situation was becoming critical. The ticking of the clock seemed to get louder with each passing minute. Seven full minutes had passed, and the doctor slid his hand up the baby's spine and turned the baby, moving the body. All at once, the baby was released lying on the table. The third stage of pregnancy is the placental expulsion, which occurs almost after the delivery of the second baby. Sutures were required, and once again, Beth and Mary were impressed with the unknown doctor's skills.

The sedation was wearing off, the patient was coming around, and she was babbling something about her babies, which convinced Beth and Mary the girl had the knowledge of multiple births. The feet prints were taken along with the completion of the birth certificates, which the doctor signed, he was snapping orders. The nurses were to prepare and clean the patient and make her ready for travel. As soon as he barked his last commandment, he was gone from the area. Mary washed the girl while fitting her with proper sanitary pads, and her gown and bed linens were changed, and she was ready for the awaiting ambulance for the return to The Lakewood Sanitarium. Beth and Mary both agreed the patient should remain for at least an hour or two to monitor her stats as she had a very rough delivery, but they weren't allowed to question the orders of the attending physician.

Two aides arrived from the sanitarium along with a well-dressed woman whom neither of the nurses knew. She checked the papers, including the foot prints, the time and dates on the birth certifications, then signed and dated the documents as well. Beth and Mary were certain the lady was from a county agency taking charge of the babies, perhaps for adoption. It was a sad ending to the whole procedure, the nurses wondered if the girl would ever see or hold her babies.

Beth and Mary's hearts were heavy as they went about cleaning the operating room, disposing of any signs that a delivery had taken place. It was now after midnight, and both nurses were tired, their task was complete. No one would ever know the secrets of operating room number 2, of The Lake View General Hospital until seventeen years later.

Coatesville, Coates, County: 1980

Coatesville was established soon after the Civil War ended in May of 1865; a debate took place every year at The Harvest Town picnic as to the founder of the town. Andrew Post owned the farmland that the town was built on, later selling the remainder of his farm to Harrison McKinny, which is still owned and operated by McKinny's Family. Avery Coates opened the first and only general store, a feed and grain mill and a very small bank, the general store was replaced by an IGM in the early nineteen sixties. The original general store is still standing and is owned and operated by McCarty's, better known as Dolly and Mac. Dolly and Mac are now in their eighties. They watched several generations of children grow to be adults, and they helped many people in the county over the years by extending credit or, on occasion, making small loans when times were lean. The old general store is still open every day except Sundays and has become more of a convenience store where some of the older retired residents can meet every day for a good cup of coffee, discuss their aches and pains, and get a healthy dose of the latest gossip.

The Coatesville Courier is published on Wednesday and Saturday, the old building that houses the newspaper office is on the main street known in the town limits as Post Road, which runs East and West. Gus Johnston is the editor who had ancestors that served in the Civil War. Anything that ever happened in the last 75 years, Gus has filed away with pictures when available. Gus could always be found with a camera at every important event within the county. Every birth, marriage, and death had its place in Gus's files, many of the prior sheriffs relied on Gus as a rich source of concise information, while he also could keep a secret. Little did Gus know one picture he would take at a special event would become very significant in changing Coatesville forever.

Every small town has a diner, and Coatesville was no exception, the locals met every morning for breakfast, between bites and sips of hot coffee, every subject was discussed. The weather, feed and grain prices, along with which couples were spatting, which couples may be, contemplating divorce, which teens were dating, the men making the trip to another county seeking entertainment and which wives were suffering from occasional abuse. One of the worst-kept secrets of the county was Honee's house, which is just over the eastern county line in Center County, it was advertised to be a gentlemen's club, but everyone, including the sheriff, knew men could get more than whiskey at Honee's. It was always a hot topic of discussion on Monday mornings, when men crossed the county line on Saturday night and how much of their weekly wages were spent for their entertainment. The latest hot topic is the coming school year with the placement of a new principal, who would be new to the community, while the people of the town are warm and friendly, new residents were always viewed with caution.

Coates County is a dry county, it is abutted on the east by Center County with a large stream, spanned by a two-laned bridge which in recent years had been widened by ten feet after two prominent residents were killed in a head-on collision. Farming is the largest business in the county, animals outnumbered the population three to one, every business relied on the farmers for their success, suffering or prosperity according to the yearly harvest yield. The sheriff of Coatesville is Henry (Buzz) O'Neil Jr. earned the nickname Buzz in grade school as his hair was cut very close in a military style. After graduation, he joined the USMC, giving him a free ticket to Vietnam in 1968. He was assigned as a door gunner on missions to retrieve wounded. Buzz should help to save lives, but if he lost even one man, he would consider the mission a failure. Buzz hated the war, he never believed there was a winner after seeing the death and destruction caused by two governments determined to destroy the other for power and control. Buzz didn't speak Vietnamese but tried to interact with the people, especially the children, he saw in the sad little faces and eyes fear and confusion, never able to trust, worrying who was friend or foe, fearful of the possibility of packing up and moving to avoid a raid or worrying if a family member would fall as a casualty. Upon returning home, Buzz learned a local boy was killed in the war, which reinforced his hatred for the war. Buzz made a vow never to leave Coatesville again or have his family touched by the horrors he had encountered during the war. In 1974, the office of sheriff was open, and Buzz filed the necessary papers to have his name placed on the ballot, he carried the county with seventy- seven percent of the vote. Buzz was a big man, standing six feet four inches without an ounce of fat. His uniform shirts stretched his biceps, while his steady gaze was enough to intimidate the most brazen teen causing trouble. There wasn't much trouble in Coates County. The teens didn't have much free time, but in the heat of the summer, they might make their way to one of the irrigation ponds on the McKinny farm, which the McKinny's didn't object to the activity; the teens were grateful and always making sure all thrash was removed, and no damage was ever done to the property. Buzz had to contend with late-night traffic stops, mostly on weekend nights when men would return from Center County driving drunk and would find themselves spending the night in the county jail. There were people in town Buzz trusted and those he didn't, he kept his ear to the ground for the slightest sign of trouble and stored in his mind every bit of information he heard, never knowing when it might be beneficial. In 1980, Buzz's instincts would be tested when a chain of events changed the town of Coatesville forever, and the peace and tranquility would become Obscured.

Chapter One: July 17th, 1980

Evonne: Woman on the Verge: page one

The Taylor home was located on Ellis Ave, it was a large two-story white structure with dark green shutters, with a covered front porch that ran the full width of the house. A large front door entry opened to a long hall with a staircase to the right leading to the second floor, the hall separated the two large front rooms. The huge kitchen with a dining area was at the rear of the house, with four large windows looking out to a well-kept lawn and large shade trees that had matured over the last thirty-five years. Dr. Roy Taylor opened his practice when the house was completed in 1945. Four years later, a son (Clark Taylor) was delivered. The house now was home to Clark and his wife of seven years, Evonne.

Dawn was breaking when Evonne awoke from a long and restless night of sleeping on the sofa; she was stiff and sore, and her body seemed unwilling to function. The room she had slept in was painted with glossy ivory, which made the sunlight streaming through the windows seem harsh to her eyes. This room used to be one of Evonne's favorite places in the house and, at one time, served as the waiting room for Dr. Taylor's thriving medical practice, while the room across the hall served as his office and examination room, now, the rooms seemed empty and useless.

Evonne was a very small woman, standing barely five feet and weighing less than a hundred pounds. She stood up, testing her legs, and started towards the hallway. She was accosted by the smell of sour liquor caused by a large spot of vomit, which had soaked into her hand-woven Peruvian rug during the night. With pure disgust, and while trying to hold her breath, Evonne sidestepped the spot and continued down the hall, entering the bathroom, thinking she could still smell the sour odor coming from the hall. She switched on the light over the wash basin, looking in the mirror, she was appalled by the image staring back, her eyes were red-rimmed and swollen, with bags under her eyes the size of half a walnut shell. There were four elongated bruises on the left side of Evonne's neck with a large bruise under her right ear lobe, all caused by the stranglehold Clark used in his latest abuse the prior night. The bruising was very visible, livid and in full purple color. Evonne usually restored to make-up as a cover, but today, no make-up would cover Clark's latest handy work. She was tired of making excuses for Clark's abuse that was occurring on a more frequent basis. The anger Evonne felt was of such intensity she feared her own actions, it was time for clear thinking and a plan.

Evonne went to the kitchen for some much-needed coffee; her head was pounding, she started the coffee and put a bagel in the toaster and was relieved, no sounds were coming from anywhere in the house. Clark must still be asleep upstairs. The large window above the kitchen sink provided a lovely view of the backyard; Evonne loved watching the squirrels and the rabbits with their newborns and, in early spring, seeing the birds building their nests with the promise of new life. Evonne started to reflect on what her life had become in the last seven years, her marriage to Clark had started with such promise, she was the new wife of a lawyer who could parlay his law background into a political career, possibly as a state senator or even governor. Clark had fallen well short of those expectations, his non-existing law practice had become a joke in the county, most people wouldn't let him handle a deed transfer. Clark hadn't generated any income in the past four years and had become a drunken sloth.

Evonne rubbed her neck and remembered the confrontation from the prior night: Evonne had spent the day with a committee of ladies making ready the house on Old Post Rd., which would house the new principal and family. The house belonged to the McKinny's but was rented to the county school board for a dollar a year, affording the perk of free housing for the position of principal. Evonne returned home at four thirty to find Clark behind the desk of his laughable law office, buried deep in a bottle of gin. Clark was surly and demanding when he was drinking, which was most of the time, he would start to drink every day soon after he brushed his teeth in the morning. Evonne was tired, the committee had spent several weeks preparing the house for residency, clearing old trunks from the attic, painting, and washing all the windows, the final touches were hanging baskets of fern and a new welcome mat at the front door. Evonne wanted a hot bath and started up the stairs completely ignoring Clark, which enraged him, he came at her with such intensity and rage, she was knocked to the floor, he grabbed her holding her up against the wall with a strangle hold, her feet were completely off the floor. Clark's face was only inches from Evonne, his hot, reeking breath made her turn her face away, he slapped her hard across her cheek and told her to look at him when he was speaking to her. The hold Clark had on Evonne was making her dizzy and she feared she would lose consciousness, with all the strength she could muster, she brought her knee up to his groin, he immediately released his hold, dropped to the floor moaning, and vomited. Evonne wasn't sure how long he had lay in the hallway as she went upstairs, and behind a locked bathroom door, she took a bath. When the water began to cool, she got out of the tub, dressed in her PJs and went downstairs. Clark was gone, and the house was quiet.

The toaster popped and brought Evonne back to the present, only to realize Clark had made his way into the kitchen, his hair was askew, and he needed a shave and bath. The alcoholism over the last four years had only become worse, Clark looked ten years older than his actual age. Evonne had little pity for the man who stood in front of her, the same man whom she promised to love, honor, and obey just seven years earlier. Evonne forgot about her bagel and coffee and pushed past Clark to go upstairs and get dressed, she had a hair appointment. Before leaving the house, she found Clark in his so-called office and reminded him of the school board meeting taking place that night and to have the spot of vomit cleaned up before she got home. Clark was a member of the school board; he was selected to do a resume check on the applicants for the Coatesville principal position. Clark was to present his findings and make his recommendation to the board at the meeting. Evonne was hoping he had enough sense to stay sober just for one day. Evonne did little that day to disguise or cover the marks of abuse. As she slammed the front door behind her, she felt vindicated, no longer blaming herself for what Clark's life had become, a man who she didn't recognize or love anymore.

The house Evonne had once loved, where she planned to start a family, had turned into a house of horror and abuse by a man she had come to despise. Clark's newest prized procession was a bright red Corvette with vanity tags that read "My Vette" which was parked in the driveway beside Evonne's modest Buick sedan, which paled in comparison. Evonne had a plan forming in her mind. Clark was running through his inheritance at an alarming rate, and she was going to make sure he didn't spend her money as well.

When Evonne and Clark were dating while still in college, they made frequent trips to Coatesville on weekends and holidays. Clark introduced her to his classmates, but the one person she had never met was Carol Furry, who owned and operated the local beauty salon. The first time Evonne met Carol, she was in awe. Carol was gorgeous, her eyes were a perfect almond shape, emerald in color, beautiful skin, full lips and a figure most men would ogle and women would mortgage their homes for. Evonne's was very non-descript, very small, with mouse brown hair, and Carol soon changed all of that. Together, they decided a honey blonde would be a good color for Evonne, Carol styled her hair to fit the contours of her face, showed Evonne make-up tips to accent her best features, and nail care between manicures. Evonne loved her new look and was very thankful she had met Carol, but she couldn't understand Carol's guarded nature in any conversation other than shop talk, it seemed Carol interacted a lot more with her other patrons. Evonne had a sixth sense when it came to reading people, but Carol was a complete puzzle. Evonne started to wonder if Carol may have been an old flame that had been jilted by Clark when he met her. As luck would have it, Evonne found the chance to ask the lingering questions about a possible romance between Clark and Carol when she saw Betsy O'Neil in the drugstore. Betsy was married to Buzz (the sheriff), and were both classmates of Clark and Carol. Betsy was very forthcoming about the subject, saying, "Carol hates Clark with passion," which stunned Evonne. Betsy told Evonne, "Clark made Carol's school days a living nightmare. There wasn't a day Carol didn't suffer from Clark's fun making, he would call her an ugly pig or hog and make rude noises, oinking or mooing, to the point Carol wouldn't participate in any class activities. Clark had the whole school joining the cruel treatment; everyone followed his lead or may find themselves the brunt of his obnoxious behavior". Betsy continued, "Buzz and I were the only two people Carol would let her guard down with, she was so miserable, I worried about her state of mind." Evonne was flabbergasted, Carol was beautiful, but Betsy explained that wasn't always the case, and Clark took full advantage of Carol's awkwardness and the less than fortune looks of a young girl. The conversation Evonne had with Betsy explained a lot about Carol's reluctance to talk about personal matters. Still, now Carol had become a close confidant, as Evonne experienced abuse from Clark on a very regular basis.

There wasn't any need for an explanation when Carol witnessed the marks on Evonne's neck upon her arrival at the hair salon. Carol's warm, welcoming smile soon changed to a mask of disgust and loathing. Carol's hatred for Clark hadn't dissipated over the years, she remembered all too well the cruelty and verbal abuse she had suffered at the hands of Clark Taylor, now it was Evonne's suffering. Evonne recounted the incident on the prior night, when she told Carol that she had kneed Clark in the groin, and Clark fell to his knees and vomited. Carol doubled over in laughter. Carol told Evonne she wished she would have known males had such a sensitive area when she was younger, because she would have kicked Clark's balls through the roof of his mouth. They were still laughing when the salon door opened and Buzz, in full uniform appeared, his large frame filled the whole doorway. Carol turned the styling chair Evonne was sitting in to face Buzz with the hope he would see the abusive marks on her neck, the trick must have worked as it seemed like Buzz lost his train of thought for an instant. Buzz regained his composure and told Carol the reason for his visit, there were reports of a Peeking Tom made to the sheriff's office on three separate occasions in the last week. The two people Buzz trusted completely, besides his deputy, were Gus at the newspaper office and Carol, both were rich sources of information. There was a much hot gossip shared at Carol's salon with the women of the area as the diner and the men, Buzz hoped Carol could spread the word about the peeking tom and women of the area would take precautions.

The discussion about the abuse ended as other patrons of the salon started to arrive. Evonne told Carol of her plans. Evonne left the salon and headed toward the main part of town; she found a parking space between the two places she wanted to visit. The first was the clinic which bore the name of her late father-in-law, Dr. Roy Taylor, all the prestige the Taylor family once held in the county Clark had managed to ruin. The clinic was the only remaining shred of respectability the Taylor name carried in the county. Evonne entered the clinic and saw Molly Paterson with her son Troy, who looked sick as a dog, waiting to see the doctor. Evonne checked with the receptionist and was told the doctor was with a patient, and Troy would be next to be seen, but Evonne was free to wait. Evonne decided to go to her second stop, which was the bank, and then return to the clinic. The bank in Coatesville was the oldest building in town, it was the standard small hometown bank, the lobby had marble floors, high windows and old polished wood. The guard was often nodding off sitting in the lobby, one teller manned the window, but Evonne wanted to see the bank president. Per Evonne's request, Mr. Stevens appeared in the lobby to escort her to his office, he was a businessman as well as the president of the Coates County School Board and very sparse on small talk. The school board was to meet that night, and Mr. Stevens had become aware of an issue he wanted to discuss with Evonne and was just getting ready to call her. Mrs. Zinn had decided to retire after 32 years as a teacher in the district, he knew Evonne had a degree in education and was wondering if she would like to fill the position. Evonne was stunned and elated, for seven years she had put her career on hold, hoping to start a family, but now those plans seemed obscure and distant, she immediately agreed. Clark was a member of the school board, Evonne feared he would vote no to the proposal, but the majority carried the vote, so she knew she had the job. Evonne learned she would be teaching the third grade, which had thirteen children enrolled for the new school year, she was so excited she almost forgot the reason for her visit to the bank. Evonne was short on small talk as well when she told the bank president the reason for her visit, Clark was spending money in a free fall mode, she knew to the penny how much of their joint account money was hers. Opening a new account wasn't something the president usually handled, but Evonne didn't want that information to be known all over the county. She transferred the precise amount of money into her new account, ordered checks in her name alone, signed the signature card, if the transaction shocked Mr. Stevens in any way, his demeanor wasn't revealing.

Evonne made her way to the clinic, when she entered, she noticed the waiting room was empty and took a seat by a window, awaiting her turn to see the doctor. She marveled at the good fortune that had befallen her and started to remember what had brought her to this point in her life.

She had met Clark Taylor when she was a senior in college, while in the library researching an essay for class, trying to reach a book on an upper shelf, she was surprised when a young man retrieved the book and handed it to her. Evonne turned to find a young man who was about a foot taller than her with an easy smile, she fumbled for words but did manage to thank him and return to her study table. He followed her, and he asked her to have a late dinner with him. Evonne wasn't interested in any kind of relationship, but she was intrigued by the handsome stranger, not to mention she was hungry. They went to a small café and talked for over two hours. Evonne was amazed with his self-assurance and his ability not to take anything too seriously, including himself. The relationship progressed and turned sexual, soon Clark moved into Evonne's off-campus apartment. There were small signs Evonne missed in his behavior at the start, now Evonne saw those traits all too clearly. The couple made several trips to Clark's hometown, Evonne found his mother to be warm, she liked her very much, while Dr. Roy Taylor was distant and aloof. All that changed when the couple visited Evonne's home in the deep northwest, a fifteen-thousand-acre tree farm. Clark had no idea of the vast wealth of Evonne's family, it seemed like overnight Clark's dad had a lot of time to spend with Evonne on their visits. Dr. Taylor would squire Evonne around town, making sure she understood the prestige and position he held in the county. Clark's attitude changed as well, and he started to question Evonne's choice of career, he couldn't understand why she wanted to be a teacher when she would inherit a sizeable fortune. Money wasn't as important to Evonne, she loved children, she wanted to contribute to the education system, and she had nothing to do with the vast wealth her family had built. Clark's manipulation was deliberate and slow. Over the next few months, he used every opportunity to belittle Evonne's choice of career, the small apartment she rented, even the car she owned. The apartment she rented, which she paid all the bills for, soon became "Their" apartment and seemed too small and seedy for Clark's taste. Their conflicting schedules of college classes allowed minimal time to spend together, the weekends provided some quiet time for the couple. One weekend in September of 1972, Evonne was preparing a large breakfast while Clark slept in, when the phone rang. Evonne assumed it was her mother calling, she answered with a chipper voice only to have a strange male on the other end ask to speak to Clark Taylor. The somber voice on the phone wasn't a "hey, how are you doing call" Evonne was told it was the sheriff of Coates County, and he needed to speak to Clark, it was urgent. She went to the bedroom to find Clark in a very deep sleep, he took the call and his expression changed from groggy to wide awake and alert after listening to the sheriff for a few minutes. The sheriff told Clark, his parents were traveling out of Coatesville, crossing the two-lane bridge that span Coates County and Center County when a large box truck coming from the opposite direction mis-judged the bridge abutment, lost control and hit his parents' car head-on, killing them both instantly. The sheriff assured Clark, his parents' death was instant, which was of little consolation to him, he informed the sheriff he would be leaving for home at once. The trip to Coatesville seemed longer than usual, the silence was almost deafening, Clark experienced emotions ranging from regret to grief to anger. The whole town and most of the county turned out for the funeral of Taylors, Evonne remained in Coatesville for two weeks before returning to college, Clark stayed to settle the estate. Clark inherited his parents' entire estate, two large life insurance policies, and a very large settlement from the trucking company responsible for his parents' death. When Clark returned to college, he had missed a full semester, his attitude had changed, the newfound wealth made his college career seem unimportant.

The subject of marriage started soon after the death of Clark's parents, when Evonne hesitated, Clark played on her sympathy, arguing he had lost his parents and he wouldn't be able to live without her. They were married in the spring of 1973 in a civil ceremony, with Evonne's parents in attendance, her life with Clark had begun. The couple graduated from college soon after the wedding and moved to Coatesville, Clark set up his law practice in the same room his father had started his medical practice. The first two years of their marriage were everything Evonne had ever hoped for, a husband she adored, his promising career, and the possibility of conceiving Clark's baby.

Evonne didn't know how long she had been musing when hearing her name being called by the receptionist in the clinic, she was told the doctor was ready for her visit. Dr. Bender was behind his desk and rose to greet Evonne, he directed her to a seat across his desk, if he noticed the abuse marks on her neck, he never mentioned it. Dr. Bender was a short, round man with unruly eyebrows that looked like metal wires jutting from his forehead, his nose was fleshy with nostrils the size of dimes. A small pair of reading glasses were always perched on his oversized nose, he gazed over the glasses and asked Evonne the reason for her visit. Dr. Bender was aware of Evonne's desire to have a child and was wondering if she was there to confirm a pregnancy. Evonne responded with, "I am going to have thirteen children," which puzzled the doctor. Evonne explained the teaching job she had been offered and the number of students enrolled for the new school year was thirteen, but the reason for her visit, she wanted a prescription for birth control pills. Evonne knew in her heart her marriage was over, the abuse on the previous night had confirmed it, now the last thing she wanted was a child with a man she hated. When Clark was drinking, he became demanding and often, their sex was more like rape, there wasn't any love or tenderness involved, even the thought of sex with him made her sick. Evonne was happy Clark made frequent trips to

Honee's House, he found whatever he needed to satisfy his ugly sexual desires, which lessened his desire for marital sex with Evonne.

The steady stare Dr. Bender had on Evonne' peeking over the bridge of his glasses, changed, he leaned back in his chair, all the questions he wanted to ask were put to rest with the tone of Evonne's voice, there was no room for discussion. He posed the usual questions: date of her last menstrual cycle, if her cycle was regular? and did she take any other medication? A full physical followed, in the end, Evonne left the clinic with a prescription for birth control pills. For a very long time Evonne had given in to the notion she was to be a shadow of her husband, seen but not heard, he slowly tried to destroy her self-esteem, but realizing today she was once again her own person.

The drugstore in Coatesville was not an option for having her prescription filled, so Evonne decided to travel into Center County, as she approached her car, she noticed Buzz was leaning up against her driver's side door, there wasn't any eluding him. "I want to have a word with you," Buzz said, Evonne wasn't in the mood to discuss her failing marriage with him as she knew he had been classmates with Clark. Buzz was just a determined, "I saw the marks on your neck, whatever goes on in your house is your business less it crosses the line, then it becomes my business." Evonne told Buzz she was late and didn't have time for this discussion, but before she could continue, Buzz interrupted, saying he only needed a minute of her time. Reluctantly Evonne told Buzz to get into her car, having no intention of discussing her abuse or her failing marriage on the sidewalk in earshot of pedestrians. Buzz took up a considerable part of the front seat but turned with his back pressed against the door so he could talk to Evonne while looking at her. "Clark and I were friends in school, but as far as my job goes, I am a sheriff first, and friendship must take a back seat. There are a few other women in the county who disappear for a couple of days due to abuse, but I can't get any of them ever to press charges against their abusers", Buzz told Evonne. "I won't press charges either," stated Evonne. Buzz was frustrated with her reply, he told Evonne that abuse usually escalated and became more frequent, and he feared for her safety, adding that Clark could do considerable damage to a person her size and weight. Evonne turned and faced Buzz, looking him right in the eyes, and said, "The harm has already been done, the damage is not repairable." Buzz saw the look in Evonne's eyes, and that look worried him.

Clark was bored with his life in a small town, he could never understand his father's desire to treat patients with boils on their backside, an occasional pregnancy, or stomach flu, when he could have made much more money in a larger area. The few times Clark patronized the diner he was usually seated next to farmers with dried mud on their boots, wanting to talk about the latest prices for cattle at auction, the pending weather, or the fluctuating milk prices. Their definition of an evening well spent was sitting on the porch and watching the sunset, Clark envisioned a far different life. Reno was a city where every vice known to man could be bought twenty-four hours a day, with bright lights and constant activity, but Clark had two major problems: money and Evonne. Clark had inherited a sizeable estate, but his money would eventually run out, but Evonne's was endless. In the beginning Clark liked Evonne well enough she seemed satisfied to give her up career with the promise of a stable home life and the prospect of having a family, but Clark knew that wasn't possible. Clark had made the mistake of impregnating a young girl while in high school, his father was furious, so to ensure an unwanted pregnancy wouldn't ever happen again, he made Clark have a vasectomy. Clark never divulged the information about the girl's pregnancy or the vasectomy before or after their marriage, if withholding those facts seemed cruel, it never occurred to Clark. A divorce was out of the question for Clark, Evonne had a lot more assets, a thought that gulled him, he was going to have to control his abusive nature, which only increased his desire to hurt her. Evonne had become a bore just like the other people in town, concerning herself with civic matters, raising money for charitable efforts, and the damn school board. Clark didn't care about the school system; he was a member of the board and was to present his recommendation to the board at the meeting. Clark received three applications for the position of principal; the one he had settled on was Mr. William Westerkamp from Boston, Massachusetts. His resume was checked, Clark patted himself on the back for a job well done.

The conversation Evonne had with Buzz was disturbing, everything he told her was true, the abuse was becoming more frequent and violent, but she was determined Clark would never hurt her again. When she arrived home, the hall rug runner was gone, Clark was in his office, he was clean-shaven, wearing a suit and tie, if he had been drinking, it was minimal. As Evonne stood in the doorway of his office, the emotional distance between them had become much greater than the physical distance between them now as they faced off, Clark told Evonne he would be taking his car to the school board meeting. The conversation wasn't necessary, Evonne assumed Clark was going to leave the meeting as soon as possible for a late-night trip to Honee's House, which she was grateful for as it meant she would spend a restful night of sleep without the fear of Clark's sexual appetite.

The Coates County school was located on Apple Ave, until 1975. One building was used for every grade one through twelve, a new building was constructed for the elementary classes, one through sixth grade, while the older building housed seventh through twelfth grades. The two buildings were connected by a very large corridor, which was used for the cafeteria, gym, and locker rooms. The school board meeting was held in the cafeteria, Mr. Stevens called the meeting to order at exactly seven o'clock. There were five members of the school board: Ty McKinny had replaced her father, who had fallen ill, Buzz's father, Henry O'Neil Sr., Dr. Thomas Bender, Clark Taylor, and Mr. Stevens, who was acting president. The school board meetings were open to the public, Gus Johnson was always in attendance with his camera, taking notes for the next issue of the local paper, throughout the year, Gus also printed the weekly meals in the cafeteria. The meeting agenda was heavy tonight, a lot of topics had to be covered, starting with the position for a new principal, the chair called Clark Taylor for his presentation. Much to everyone's surprise, Clark was well prepared and precise, he reminded Evonne of the young man she had met in college. He informed the board that he had received three resumes for the position, that he had checked each candidate thoroughly, and his recommendation was William Westerkamp from Boston Massachusetts. Mr. Westerkamp was a retired Army officer, he had a four-year degree in education, he spoke two foreign languages fluently, Spanish and Italian, he was married to one boy who would be a senior, and he was very interested in physical education. Mr. Westerkamp currently held a position at a prestigious co-ed prep school in Boston; Clark told the board he had concerns as to why Mr. Westerkamp would want to leave a job with a lucrative salary to accept a position with considerably lower pay. Clark assured the board he had explored that issue with a phone call. Mr. Westerkamp told Clark he was born in a small town in Kansas, he had traveled all over the world in war and peacetime, that he had moved every time the Army reassigned him, and he was looking for a small town with peace and quiet. Having finished his presentation, Clark turned to Mr. Stevens and said, "I hereby resign as a member of the Coates County School Board, effective immediately," he put the resume on the table, picked up his briefcase and left the room. The remaining board members, as well as the people attending the meeting stared after Clark in disbelief, Evonne wasn't surprised, she knew Clark had very little interest in anything but Clark. The board would have to place a new member before the rest of the meeting's agenda could be conducted. Mr. Stevens was quick with a solution, a man who attended every meeting, who knew as much about the workings of the school board as any regular member, Gus Johnson. Gus was pleased and honored; he replaced Clark at the table, and the meeting continued. Mr. Westerkamp was named as the new principal; the second order of business was the proposal for Evonne Taylor to fill the position as third-grade teacher in the wake of Mrs. Zinn's retirement, Evonne was asked to leave the room while the vote took place, after the vote was over and Evonne returned to the meeting, she had a new job. Two minor issues were brought to the floor: there was an opening in the cafeteria, which would be filled locally, and the approval for Wendy Whitfield to maintain the school supply closet. The next school board meeting would be scheduled for the second Tuesday in August at Seven O'clock and the meeting was adjourned.

Evonne wanted to talk to Ty McKinny after the meeting, Ty's father was in failing health, and everyone in town knew it was only a matter of time. The stress was telling on Ty's face, she had been placed at the helm of a thousand-acre dairy farm, with a pending death in her family, Evonne wanted to say something, but words seemed inadequate. Evonne left the meeting with a heavy heart, she hoped Clark wouldn't be at home, she didn't care where he was at, who he was with, or what time he would stagger in the house if he left her alone.

Chapter Two Carol: Ugly duckling to beautiful swan

Every aspect of Carol's childhood was ugly, she couldn't understand how she had missed out on the beauty that surrounded her. Her father (Jack) was brawny with dark hair, a sharp chiseled jaw, and clear pale green eyes, her mother (Ruby) was a full-bodied woman and beauty that couldn't be enhanced with make-up. Carol had a brother who was five years younger, with the combination of his parents' good looks, while she was an ugly duckling. Jack left the family when Carol was nine years old, she always blamed herself for his abrupt departure and would often look at her third-grade picture to affirm the fact. The picture was a fat-faced girl with freckles across her nose and chubby checks, mouse-brown hair cut in a bowl shape, and large square adult teeth that were much too big for a child's face, which earned her the cruel name of "Buggy" in reference to the cartoon character Bugs Bunny, by her classmates. Carol often thought it would have been better if her father was dead, her mother spent many nights crying as if she were in mourning, Carol would also lay awake and mourn for a man she loved and hated at the same time. There were only a few bright spots in Carol's young life, and one was her brother, Mike, she adored the time spent with the cheerful little boy who returned her love in full measure despite her ugliness. Ruby took a job at the diner to support the family, but Carol often wondered if her father was sending money, they lived a much better lifestyle than a small salary and tips would provide. It was Carol's job to stop at the babysitter's house and pick up Mike after school, it didn't matter how much torment she endured at school, Carol found refuge with Mike's love.

The hurt and humiliation Carol suffered at school was relentless, day after day she was forced to endure being singled out as the focus of amusement. Clark Taylor was the instigator, every person who wanted to be in his circle of friends followed his lead, if they didn't, they would find themselves being the brunt of one of his bad jokes. Carol tried to avoid any situation where Clark could put on a spectacle at her expense, she didn't participate in any school activities, the worst part of her day was lunchtime. Before the cafeteria was built each student had to bring their lunch to school, on nice days, the kids were allowed to go outside and eat on the lawn. Clark never missed an opportunity to remind the whole class that Carol was overweight by making rude noises, like oinking and mooing, and telling her there wasn't a bag big enough for her lunch. Carol often would have her lunch behind a locked door in a toilet stale of the girl's bathroom, sitting on a commode with her lunch on her lap. The days seemed endless, the verbal abuse heartless, and her hatred over helming for Clark Taylor.

The anger Carol had was accelerating, the humiliation was heartbreaking, and her ability to function was waning, just when she thought things couldn't get any worse, she was proven wrong. At the age of thirteen, Carol was in the stage between a child and a young adult, she was entering the ninth grade, not much had changed over the summer except she experienced her first menstrual cycle. The class was to vote on officers for the school year, the teacher had listed each office on the board with the names of the nominees, the voting was to be held the next day. Carol entered the classroom to find everyone laughing hysterically, indicating that she should look at the blackboard, there had been a new office listed, Mascot for the FFA (Future Farmers of America), Carol Furry was the only nominee. Carol was completely broken and devastated, she somehow managed to get to her seat, trying to act unfazed while feeling like she wanted to crawl away and die. When the teacher came into the room and saw the commotion, she demanded to know who was responsible, but the damage was done. Carol knew it was Clark Taylor, and she silently vowed her revenge. Carol didn't participate in the voting, all she could manage to do was hang her head and try to disappear, as soon as the bell rang to change classes, she gathered her books and walked out of the school, determined never to return. The misery Carol felt continued as she made her way home from school. Mike was in the third grade now and wouldn't be at home to offer his love, she cursed her life and her looks. Carol entered through the backdoor leading into the kitchen, hurling her books across the room, hitting the wall with such an impact that it knocked the figurines off the shelf next to the dining table. She slammed her body onto a chair, knowing she couldn't hurt herself any worse than the hurt she had just experienced at school, clenching her teeth until she tasted blood, her hands were drawn into fists with her fingernails cutting into her palms, and she started to scream. The screams turned into deep agonizing sobs, while her body rocked back and forth, until her energy was spent. Carol lost track of time and didn't know how long she had sat there when she heard the back door open, it was her mother, she received a call from the school informing her that Carol had left school after her first class. Mrs. Blair was worried about Carol and offered her deepest apology for the incident, she explained to Ruby while on the phone the depth of Clark Taylor's obnoxious behavior and exactly what had happened to cause Carol to leave school. Ruby sat down opposite Carol, waiting for her to acknowledge her presence, the silence hung between them for a long time, Ruby's heart was bleeding at the sight of her daughter, in that instant, Ruby also felt the same hate Carol had. Carol finally looked at her mother and begged her not to make her ever return to school, Ruby remained calm and asked Carol a simple question, "Do you think I'm pretty"? The question stunned Carol, her mother was the most beautiful woman in town, an opinion shared by many men, all that would have been glad to fill Jack Furry's shoes. Ruby left the table, when she returned, she placed a photo on the table, Carol was puzzled, the picture looked like her third-grade picture, but the photo was too old. The photo showed a solemn-faced young girl with chubby cheeks, an unflattering hairstyle, and freckles across the nose. The girl in the photo is me, Ruby said, the same transformation that happened to me will also happen to you, Mother Nature takes her time on beauty, the girls you envy now will one day envy you, I promise. Ruby told Carol, "Remember, a pretty dish is nothing if the dish is empty."

Carol went back to school, almost from the start she noticed changes, not in her appearance, but in her heart, soul, and determination, she wasn't a shrinking violet, the first people to recognize the changes were her teachers. She was asked to write a column in the class paper, which thrilled Carol as her dream was to become a journalist, she held her head high, not as a form of arrogance, but pride. Carol started to participate in every class activity, she attended school dances, and little by little, a few of her female classmates were accepting her. For the first time, she was eating lunch with a couple of girls on the lawn. The transformation had started, her appearance hadn't changed much, she did notice she was developing breasts and her waist was slimming, but her world was expanding, she had a few friends, and her school life was exciting and fun. The one aspect of Carol's life that didn't change was her hatred for Clark Taylor, she was patient, bidding her time for the day the transformation her mother promised was complete. Carol's thirst for revenge was palatable, she had figured out Clark's Achilles Heel, his ego, when Carol finally acquired her mother's beauty, her plan for Clark would destroy him.

Vietnam: JULY 1980, LITTLE GIRL LOST

The night was falling, darkness finally engulfed Sueme, she was ready to embark on the final leg of her journey, traveling only at night to avoid detection. The trip had taken Sueme two weeks of careful planning, she had been gone for forty-eight hours, and she knew her uncles would be looking for her, it was more important than ever to remain out of sight. Sueme's mother had died a year ago, she resided with her uncles, her bedroom had a filthy mattress on the floor, and one light hanging from the ceiling, with a tattered curtain hanging in the doorway. Sueme's uncles sold the young girl into day slavery and prostituted her at night. Several men would visit her each night with whiskey breath and reeking body odors. Sueme was hopeful she could reach her destination by morning, the few provisions she had packed had run out earlier in the day, her legs were covered with abrasions, which were burning and oozing. The dress she was wearing was in shreds, but it made her bathroom stops easier and quicker, she had a small handbag that once belonged to her mother across her shoulder. The handbag was crescent-shaped canvas, with gold fringe, and a long-braided strap. Sueme hoped the contents of the bag would save her life and set her free. Sueme's energy was starting to wane from being on consent alert and wary of capture. Returning home wasn't an option she wanted to explore. Every couple of yards, she would scan her surroundings and listen for anything rustling in the bushes, she didn't fear what lay ahead, but she dreaded what she had left behind. The darkness made it impossible to discern the amount of time she had traveled, but her heart was starting to grow weary, thinking she should be seeing some signs of lights and her destination. Suddenly, her heart lurched, in the distance, she saw what looked like small twinkling dots of light; she wanted to break into a full run to what would provide her with safety, but she had to remain alert. The twinkling dots were becoming brighter and larger, moving closer, but still on alert for danger, she stopped in her tracks when she heard noises. The noises were close, she scanned the area to find a figure digging in rubbish cans, fearing detection she dropped to her knees. The figure didn't see Sueme and continued with his search, content with his findings, the figure moved on. Scanning the area, Sueme was sure she was alone and moved on, she knew instantly she had found her destination and crept closer to find a three-foot retaining wall. Sueme climbed up on the wall, opened the lid of a large garbage dumpster, jumped in and pulled the lid down, to find herself surrounded by darkness. The stench didn't bother her, she felt safe, she settled in a corner, not caring what she may be sitting on, and she slept.

Sueme woke to another generous heap of garbage being dumped, almost on top of her, the lid closed, but she could tell dawn had broken. The garbage yielded a few pieces of bread and a carton half full of milk, she ate and planned her next move. She pushed the dumpster lid up and peeked out, the rear entrance of the large two-story stone building was in sight, but

Sueme knew she had to enter the front door. It seemed to be about nine o'clock by the placement of the sun. Sueme pulled herself up, set her feet on the retaining wall and jumped to the ground. The front of the building had a large set of double doors. She walked up the steps and rang the bell, and she hoped someone inside would listen to her story.

Major Margret Starr was sitting at her desk having her breakfast, checking her agenda for the day, there was a staff meeting at thirteen hundred hours, but the rest of the day seemed ordinary. Margret was a career military, she was an Army nurse stationed in Vietnam at the time of the war, the decisions she made were made in a split second and would often determine if a soldier would go home alive and well or in a casket. The buzzer on Margret's desk rang, and she assumed it was a delivery in the kitchen, but it was the front door, and she heard a commotion coming from the foyer. Margret saw a young girl being retained by the private standing guard, upon seeing Margret, the girl broke loose, ran to her and threw her arms around Margret's waist. The private went after the girl, but Margret told him to stand down, she wasn't sure what had brought the girl to her, but it was a story she wanted to hear.

The girl's clothes were in rags, her shoes were barely holding together. Margret tilted the young girl's head and looked at the dirty face, the only clean area was the streaks left by tears, she realized, today was going to be anything but ordinary. Margret took the young girl to her private quarters, the first order of business was a bath, the girl didn't speak English, but when Margret showed her the tub, the girl understood. The young girl didn't show any modesty and stripped her old clothes off, but she was very protective of the handbag she carried. Margret called for a translator and a doctor, she went to her closet for clothing, she opted for a white shirt, and a pair of panties, she tapped on the bathroom door and placed the clean clothing next to the tub. Margret ordered breakfast, eggs, toast, juice, milk and jam, the meal was delivered just as the young girl emerged from her bath, the shirt looked more like a dress, but the clothing was the least of Margret's worries. The young girl spotted the hot breakfast and looked at Margret. Margret indicated for the girl to sit and eat, no translation was necessary, the girl ate as if she was starved. The translator arrived, he sat opposite the girl, and the conversation began, the girl dumped the contents of her handbag on the table, the bag held a few coins, a photo, and a pill, the conversation was rapid coming from the girl. Margret didn't speak a lot of Vietnamese, but she kept picking up on the word Nguoi cha (father), the expression on the translator's face didn't need any translation, his face changed from disbelief to horror, and then anger.

When the conversation ceased between the girl and the translator, he directed the conversation to Margret, the girl's name is Sueme, she is thirteen years old, her mother died a year ago, she was placed in the custody of two uncles, the uncles sold her for day slavery, and prostituted her at night, she had run away three days ago. The translator told Evonne the coins were stolen from her uncles because she thought she had earned them, the picture was an American soldier which Sueme believed was her father, according to her mother, and the pill was cyanide. Margret was stunned, not by the possibility the American soldier in the photo could be her father, that scenario happened more often than the Army wanted to acknowledge, what stunned her was the fact the girl had a cyanide pill in her procession. The translator explained the girl had been taught by her mother, who had lived through the war, that it was better to determine your fate rather than be taken hostage by an enemy, and if she must return to her uncles, she is fully prepared to take the cyanide. Margret told the translator to assure Sueme she was safe and to rest on her bed, Sueme slept for the next six hours. The first call Margret made was to the Department of Defense at the Pentagon in Washington, DC. She wasn't sure if the man in the photo was alive or dead, or if it was Sueme's father, but the Army would have to investigate the claims. The picture of the American soldier and Sueme's blood type would be sent, if the facts were verified, Sueme would be a ward of the Army, but Margret knew she would never allow the young girl to return to the situation she had fled from.

Carol Continued:

A series of events occurred during Carol's sophomore year in college while studying to become a journalist, her lifelong dream. Carol's mother was diagnosed with Multiple sclerosis, a chronic progressive disease- causing damage to the nerve cells in the brain and spinal cord. The symptoms are barely noticeable with the onset of the disease but rapidly cause impaired speech, muscular incoordination, blurred vision and severe fatigue, Carol didn't hesitate to drop out of college and return home. Mike was a sophomore in high school and Carol started to shoulder the responsibilities of caring for mother, running the household, and continuing to provide a stable life for her brother at the age of twenty. The burdens became heavier as Ruby's disease was reaching its final stages, Carol made peace with impending death, the pain her mother was suffering was hard to watch. Ruby Furry died in February of nineteen sixty-nine, Carol, though she was prepared, the reality painted a much different picture, the only consolation she found was her mother wasn't suffering any longer.

In the aftermath of Ruby's death Carol was left to settle the estate, the will was simple, the Children got the house, and a small insurance policy. Jack Furry wasn't mentioned in the will, but Carol did find out what she had suspected as a child, Jack (her father) was sending large support checks every month. A closet in Ruby's bedroom was very reveling, boxes of letters from Carol's father, with greeting cards for Carol and Mike for every occasion. For one reason or another, Ruby had decided not to share the cards and letters with her children, the messages in the letters were written by a man who loved his children very much. Carol became angry, if she had been given the opportunity to read his words, she would have reached out to him with return letters and cards, as much as she wanted to hate him as a child, she loved him and desperately missed him.

Returning to college wasn't an option for Carol, she now had full custody of Mike, as well as her life to do something productive, she weighed her options. The one business Coatesville didn't have was a beauty salon, the closest salon was thirty miles away, Carol formed a plan. She enrolled in a Vocational School in a neighboring county for cosmetology, which allowed her to be home with Mike in the evenings. Carol didn't want her shop in the house, so she paid a visit to Sam McKinny, he had a mobile home which at one time was used to house seasonal laborers. She offered him what she considered a fair price. Sam considered the price and said no. He told Carol she could have the trailer, and he would move it for her, Carol was thrilled, she was on her way to being a businesswoman. Carol went to school during the day and spent every available hour repairing and cleaning, she built a ramp to accommodate any older clientele her business might attract, she washed the siding and painted the shutters, at every stage of the restoration, she took pictures. The interior layout was perfect, the kitchen was in the front, she would be able to take her meals there as well as offer coffee to her patrons, the living room area would be used for her shop area, she had a wash station installed, two commercial dryers, and a manicure table. The small bedroom was used for a washer and dryer, and storage area for supplies, while the large bedroom was Carol's office area. After Carol graduated from cosmetology school, she was ready to hang her shingle, she called her salon (Permanent Solution).

July 18th, 1980

Fridays were Carol's busiest day of the week, today wasn't an exception, the speculation about Clark's resignation from the school board, Evonne's acceptance and approval for the teaching position to replace Mrs. Zinn, and the new principal, William Westerkamp from Boston Massachusetts were the hot topics throughout the day. Carol finally had a moment to grab a sandwich and make the phone call she was dreading. Sam McKinny was dying, he was very dear to Carol as he was partially responsible for success over the last ten years. Sam McKinny didn't let the vast wealth spoil him, he was generous with his money, a member of the Coates County School Board, and a good friend to everyone, but you would usually find Sam in work clothes, in the barn or working his fields, he would be sorely missed by the whole community.

Carol hired a high school girl (Wendy Whitfield) to help in the shop, Carol was good with a comb, but her organizational skills were terrible, she had a storage room that looked like a beauty supply company blew up, and her office looked like a tornado had hit a bookstore. Wendy changed all that, not only did she organize the storage room and straighten out Carol's finances, but she filled a void in Carol's life. Carol was engaged to be married to Tom Floras, but he was a cross-country trucker and was only home between runs, Mike had joined the Air Force after he graduated high school and was stationed in Texas, Carol and Wendy had formed a very close bond. Wendy was a beautiful girl, she would be entering the senior class in the fall, she wanted to study finance and leave for college after graduating from high school, which tugged at Carol's heart as she knew she would never see Wendy again. Wendy had one major problem, her father, Rev. Leroy Whitfield.

Carol was ready to close her shop and head to the house when she heard the salon door open, she gasped at the sight of her visitor, standing before her was her father, Jack Furry. The range of emotions Carol was feeling started to tumble over one another: anger, surprise, love, joy, and hate, she was speechless. Jack was looking at her like he was seeing a ghost, he said "My god, you are the image of your mother. You are a beautiful woman with a successful business. I'm so proud of you." Carol recovered from her shock, she was angry, "What are you doing here, you didn't want to bother with me as a child when you ran out on the family, why bother now"? Carol knew she wasn't being fair after she read the letters she found, but every hurt she had ever felt about his departure came pouring out. She asked him a question that had been burning in her mind since he left, "did you leave the family for another woman"? "No, Carol, I never loved another woman, no one could ever take her place, I didn't leave you willingly, your mother sent me away, do you know what the people in town called me, Black Jack, there were times I would gamble my whole pay away before I would get home on Friday, and your mother would have to make do without money. I would always promise I wouldn't gamble anymore, but the temptation was too great, it became too great of a burden for her, she told me to leave and not to return until I was ready to be a husband and father. I went to work on the pipeline, I finally stopped gambling, but by then, so much time had passed, I was afraid I would disrupt your lives, and I always worried the old habits would return and I would have to leave again, causing you the same hurt again. It was better I stayed away, but you, Mike, and your mother were always the love of my life." Carol knew he was sincere, it all made sense now, she flew into his arms, and they cried together.

Jack stroked her hair, soothed away her hurt, and promised never to leave her again, they talked for hours. She told him about her engagement, she explained how she got started in cosmetology, how Evonne was suffering from Clark's abuse, Mike joined the Air Force, Sam McKinny's illness, and about Wendy. Jack shared his plans with Carol, he was planning to start a trucking company in Coatesville, the farmers in the area paid high transportation charges for shipment of the cattle and crops. Carol marveled at her father's knowledge of business and his common sense, just as Carol had realized the practicality of a hair salon, in Coatesville, her father saw an opportunity that would serve the needs of the farmers and be profitable. The money Jack had saved while working on the pipeline was substantial, except for the money he had sent Ruby every month, he was able to save large portions of his pay. Carol was as excited about the new venture as her father. She told her father her boyfriend was a cross-country trucker, Carol hoped with a local trucking company, Tom would be home much more often. Carol and Jack finally made their way to the house. Jack took one of the spare bedrooms, Carol had her father back, and suddenly, the house didn't seem as empty and lonely.

Tyler McKinny Miller: Poor Little Rich Girl:

Sam McKinny died on July 20th, 1980. He had suffered a stroke in February of 1980, a Cerebrovascular Accident, according to the diagnosis provided by the doctor. The debilitating stroke left his face contorted, with a hideous grin, his left arm and leg were like useless appendages, and the once robust man was reduced to surrendering his dignity. Tyler suffered every day, watching a man she relied on all her life endure the humiliation of being bathed and his soiled clothes changed like an infant, he begged Ty every day to let him die.

July 24th: 1980

Sam McKinny was laid to rest on his beloved farm. Ty had heard the story of Harrison McKinny, her great-great-great grandfather, who left his family after the famine in Ireland and headed to what was known as The New World. Harrison left Middleton, working his way across the country, picking up jobs to earn money. When he reached the coast, he had the equivalent of seven dollars and fifty cents in American currency. The cost of his passage was five dollars, which afforded him a three by eight feet space, along with ninety-nine other passengers in the boat's hull. The light was minimal, the trap doors on the deck level were left open during the day, but at night, it was pitch black, less than an hour into the voyage, over half of the people in the hull were sick from the constant rocking of the boat. The sanitary conditions were deplorable, two large troughs were used to relieve bodily functions, there were rats everywhere, in the silence of the night, they could be heard gnawing. Impure water was passed out, that caused dysentery, one pound of food was given to each passenger per day, which was a weak potato soup or porridge. On several occasions, a crew member would take a woman to their quarters at night, returning her in the morning, any man who objected would be wiped when a passenger died, the body was thrown overboard. Harrison noticed the old woman next to him. She looked to be his mother's age with pure white hair and a hunch back, he shared his hopes and dreams in The New World with her, and she shared her food with him. Seventy-two passengers survived the trip; those who remained were hustled off the boat, and the baggage was thrown onto the dock in a large pile. The daylight was blinding, it took Harrison's eyes a while to adjust, while his legs regained their strength, he spotted the old woman digging for her bag. Harrison hurried over to assist her before someone made off with her luggage.

Harrison was stunned by the activity on the dock, knowing he would have to get a job, he spotted a sign advertising for able body men for dock work, he would begin working the next day. The next order of business, finding a cheap boarding house, he and the old lady started toward the shabby side of town. Harrison felt protective of the woman, at least until she got settled. The woman saw a sign advertising a bed and bath with one meal a day, together they headed in the direction of the advertised house, when they were out of sight of the dock, the woman stopped and removed her coat, it revealed a well-constructed hump sewn in the lining, she combed the talcum powder from her hair, and wiped her face, the fine lines which appeared to be from aging, disappeared. Grace was her name, she told Harrison it was a precaution, she was aware of the plight of women traveling alone. Harrison laughed until his sides were sore, he knew he would never be without Grace again no matter what the New Country held in store.

Grace was an experienced seamstress and was able to get a job in a shop making garments for the well-placed women in the area, Harrison worked the docks, they were married, after a year, they saved enough money to buy a team of horses and a wagon, they started West. Twenty-two months after Harrison left Ireland, he found a very run-down farm belonging to a man named Post, the price was one hundred dollars, he and Grace were home. Ty had been told that story at a very early age, it didn't have a deep, profound meaning until her father became ill and died.

The funeral was the biggest ever held in the county, after the services were complete, the whole town came to Ty's house carrying trays of every kind of food for what was called a (Wake), a celebration of life. Many of the residents owed their success to Sam, Henry O'Neil Sr. was the first to speak, he related how Sam had financed the start-up cost of his feed and grain mill; Carol's tribute brought tears, she talked of Sam's generosity, giving her the trailer that had become very successful over the last decade. Ty was exhausted when the last guest gave their condolences and said goodnight, leaving only Brant and his father.

Brant and Ty were to be married in August, the match was so obvious to everyone except Ty for many years. Brant Miller was born on the McKinny farm, he was the son of Bill Miller a lifelong friend and farm hand of Sam's and had become Ty's salvation when her father had fallen ill. The farm had expanded from the ten acres Harrison had bought for one hundred dollars to a thousand acres dairy farm, of which Ty was the sole survivor.

Ty was a spoiled brat as a child, from the time she was born Sam pampered her, she never heard the word no, or had a single household or farm chore, she learned to ride a horse about the same time she started to walk. Sam was unable to keep stable hands, Ty was demanding and rude with the hands on the farm, and nothing ever suited her, Sam found himself replacing stable hand about three times a year. Ty had little interest in the farm, she had an older brother who would one day assume the responsibilities of the farm's daily operation. Her brother (Sonny) was twelve years older than Ty, he was killed in a farming accident when he was twenty-one, Ty was only nine, she heard a scream coming from the barn, the screams sounded like a wounded animal, she raced to the barn area to see her mother, Sonny was on the ground in a crumpled position, he had fallen from the hay loft and broke his neck, he was dead before medical aid could arrive. In a sense, her mother died that day as well, she never recovered from the grief, she was lost in a world of the past and never ventured outside the house again. The eyes Ty remembered dancing with joy became bottomless pits of a tormented soul. Her mother's appearance was that of a very old woman. The garden her mother loved so well went to seed, the tapestry loom, which had been in the family for generations, sat with a half-completed piece never to be finished. It was less than a year after Sonny's death, Ty's mother took to her bed, asking for nothing, and not responding to any conversation. It was two years almost to the day of Sonny's death, Ty's mother died, if medically possible, of a broken heart. She was found dead in her bed holding a picture of Sonny, the picture was buried with her, and from that time on it was Ty and her father.

Ty eloped with a young farmhand at the age of eighteen, the ink on the license was barely dry, the marriage lasted two weeks until her husband was drafted and sent to Vietnam, where he was killed. Ty never had a purpose in life, she was self-indulged, after being a wife, she started to take on the household responsibilities and became involved with the financial aspect of operating a massive farm business.

Ty had no idea of the total worth of her father's estate until the lawyer opened the will, the amount was considerable, it had all started with Harrison McKinny and his vision, and now Ty wanted to make her ancestors proud. There were areas in the community that were lacking by normal standards, she donated enough money to buy a new pumper truck for the Coatesville Fire Company, she also took her father's place on the Coatesville school board.

Ty was excited about her coming marriage to a man she loved, a father-in-law she adored and the prospect of having children, she was thirty-two years old, and her biological clock was ticking. Brant and Ty were to be married in the courthouse in Center County, Carol Furry and Bill Miller would be in attendance, the ceremony would be Friday, August 1st, 1980.

Wednesday July 30th, 1980

July in Coatesville was hot and humid, every window in the house was open, and there wasn't enough of a breeze blowing to ruffle the curtains visibly. The room was a pastel yellow with exposure to the north and east, it was a perfect room for a nursery, the walls were covered with ABC blocks, lambs, ribbons and bows. In the corner was an oversized rocking chair, handcrafted by Evonne's father from the finest wood the northwest offered, seated in the rocker was a large stuffed white teddy bear with a big red bow. Evonne's parents were thrilled to know their daughter and son-in-law wanted to start a family, they made a surprise trip to bring the rocker, which was five years ago. Now the room's purpose seemed useless, even the teddy bear with its coy smile seemed to know what had taken Evonne her whole married life to realize there wouldn't be a baby for the Taylors in this room, at one time that would have devastated Evonne, now it was a blessing.

The nursery was equipped with a twin bed. Evonne had read every book on infants and childcare available, one suggestion was an extra bed for the nursery in case the baby was restless or ill now this was Evonne's bedroom. Evonne's plans were coming together, she was able to buy a house from an estate sale, the house was located on Beyers Ave., the structure was sound, but it needed major modernization, the settlement closing would be in August. She was looking forward to her new position, she visited the classroom, which was now her classroom, she labeled each desk with a student name enrolled for the third grade, a big wooden apple her father made, was placed on her desk along with a silver framed picture of her parents. The Westerkamp's had arrived from

Boston and settled into the house Evonne helped make ready, she received a note from Mrs. Westerkamp thanking her for her efforts, the family was very pleased with the residence. The Westerkamp's would be formally introduced to the community at the August school board meeting, Gus printed an article in the paper, encouraging parents to attend.

Evonne was very happy, she wasn't sure if Clark had discovered her money was missing from their account or if he knew she had purchased a house, she just started to doze off, and suddenly Clark was on top of her, ripping her nightgown, and groping her, she could smell his hot alcohol breath making it impossible to breathe. Evonne managed to turn to her side, with all the force in her legs, she pushed him over the edge of the bed onto the floor. Clark hit the floor hard, he was stunned for a second but soon came at Evonne with a vengeance, she had to think fast. Clark was very drunk, and she hoped that would even the odds. The thought of having sex with Clark not only made her sick, but angered her as well, with the heel of her palm, she slammed Clark in the nostrils, and blood splattered over the bed, Clark staggered out of the nursey mumbling something about her being as good a dead.

The house was quiet, a sense of foreboding engulfed Evonne, knowing there would be a next time for the abuse she suffered. Staying wasn't an option, she packed clothing and personal items and headed to Carol's house. The emotional state of Evonne became apparent upon her arrival when she nearly collapsed in Jack's arms, the relief of being safe was overwhelming, she began to sob uncontrollably. Jack was residing with Carol until he could find his own place. Tom, Carol's fiancé had a two-day layover from his cross-country trucking job, but Jack was more than happy to sleep on the sofa. Evonne was very tired and weary, for the first time in many months, her fears subsided, sleep came quickly, it wasn't until six o'clock she heard Tom's big Kenworth diesel pulling out of the drive.

Thursday July 31st, 1980

At seven o'clock, Evonne finally made her way to the kitchen to find Carol, Jack and Buzz having coffee, Carol had called Buzz, voicing her concern, the group listened as Evonne relived the nightmare of abuse. Buzz suggested a restraining order, Clark was spiraling out of control, Evonne agreed to the order, it was hard to say what Clark might do when he found out about the money and the house she purchased. Buzz spoke of the young Clark he had known in high school. While he was mean and obnoxious, Buzz never thought Clark would become an abusive drunk, Evonne's abuse proved Buzz wrong. Jack was angry, he told the story about Clark's father (Roy) and the brutal fights between the two of them, more than a couple of times, and Jack had to set Roy Taylor straight. Carol wanted to know what caused the fighting, Jack told her the fighting was all about Carol's mother, both men were in love with Ruby. Carol asked her father how it all ended, Jack looked at Carol and said, "I married her, didn't I?" laughter erupted at the table. Carol had to get to the shop, her first appointment was due at nine o'clock, Buzz was heading back to the office to prepare a restraining order against Clark, and Jack was heading to the diner. Jack was spending a lot of time at the diner. Carol wondered if it had anything to do with the waitress, Nan, she was older than Carol but younger than Jack.

When Buzz returned to his office from Carol's house, the phone was ringing, his deputy took the call and indicated it was for Buzz. Brant Miller was on the line to make Buzz aware of an incident at the irrigation lake, a duck was found with a broken neck hanging on a fence post. Brant told Buzz that if any more damage was done at the lake, he would post No Trespassing signs, and the lake would be off-limits to the teens in the area. Buzz was perplexed, he had never had any trouble with the teens in the area, first a peeking tom being reported, now this morbid incident, Buzz was starting to get an ominous feeling. Buzz started to fill out the form for a restraining order, it wasn't ten minutes until Clark came bristling into the sheriff's office, completely ignoring the deputy at the front desk and informed Buzz, he wanted to press charges against Evonne for spousal abuse. It was hard for Buzz to maintain a straight face when he saw the damage to Clark's face, inflicted by such a small woman, both of his eyes were black and blue, with a bandage across his swollen nose. Buzz looked at Clark without empathy, he could hardly recognize the very popular boy from high school, he looked twenty years older than his actual age because of his hard drinking. The pleasure Clark had derived from cruel remarks, bad jokes at others' expense, and the need to be the center of attention, Buzz now recognized as Narcissism, and it was becoming dangerous. Buzz remembered a time in high school, Clark was the butt of a joke, the fury and swift retaliation he displayed was almost frightening. Buzz no longer liked the man sitting across from him but had to listen to Clark's complaint. Having heard from Evonne and her accusations of self-defense, he didn't think Clark had a leg to stand on. If sex is not consented to by both parties, whether married or not, it is considered Rape, the victim has the right to defend themselves, and that was Evonne's claim.

Buzz let Clark know if he were to press charges, it would mean a court hearing and the possibility of having the whole county know what Evonne had done to him, and he might be the one found guilty. The restraining order was on Buzz's desk, he told Clark it was against him, being filed on Evonne's behalf, any further contact with her would violate the order, and he would be arrested. Clark was angry, he counted on a friendship that no longer existed, he picked up his sunglasses and stormed out of the sheriff's office. Buzz made a mental note to keep an eye on Clark's activities and Evonne's safety.

Friday August 1st, 1980

Dawn had broken, it was a beautiful day, Carol was in her shop early with limited hours. She was going to be attending the marriage of Brant Miller and Ty McKinny at the Center County courthouse. Ty was pretty with a wholesome look, she arrived early for her appointment, it was clear to Carol. Ty was a nervous wreck. Carol decided on an up-sweep style with tiny white daisies woven through the hair, Ty's nails were manicured, a pale pink polish was applied, a small amount of base and blush was applied, her brows were shaped, and mascara completed the picture, when Ty left the salon, she was radiant.

The wedding ceremony was held in judge Kreb's chambers at two o'clock, with Bill (Brant's father) and Carol standing by the bride and groom. Brant Miller looked handsome, he wore a white shirt with a stand-up collar, blue jeans, a good pair of cowboy boots, he had removed his Stetson hat for the ceremony, his father, Bill, looked on with pride on his face. Ty had chosen a simple pink cotton dress with shoestring straps, her shoes were white pumps, a single strand of pearls, which had belonged to her mother, was the only jewelry she wore. The bride and groom were gazing into each other eyes when the judge asked Brant to make his statement of commitment, Brant promised to love from this day forward a girl he had loved since he was a very young man, Ty, in a choked voice, promised the love she felt for Brant would only strengthen as they aged. Carol stared at the faces of two people, oblivious to everything but this moment in time. The rings were exchanged with vows by both the bride and groom, to love, honor, and obey, the judge pronounced the couple as man and wife, and Brant kissed Ty with love and tenderness, the couple was now Mr. and Mrs. Brant Miller. Carol was overcome with emotion, as she and Bill hugged and congratulated the couple, the small bouquet Ty carried was passed to Carol, Ty reminded Carol it was now her turn to be married.

No one in the county was aware of the nuptials that had taken place between Brant and Ty, Ty was worried some people might think the marriage was too soon after the death of her father, Carol knew different, Sam McKinny would be the first to offer the couple his blessings. It was almost five o'clock before Carol got back to the Permanent Solution salon, she wasn't surprised to find Wendy was still there, Wendy hated her home life with her overbearing father, Reverend Leroy Whitfield. Wendy was a beautiful seventeen-year-old girl, she was five feet seven inches in her bare feet, she had deep chestnut hair, blue eyes, and C-cup breasts, which didn't go unnoticed, people couldn't understand how she could be the product of the loveless marriage of Betty and Rev. Leroy Whitfield. Carol had attended a few services conducted by the Rev., his sermons were dark, hell, fire, and damnation, usually directed to women, it was a sharp contrast to the teaching Carol had received while in Sunday School as a young girl. Wendy was expected to pay tithing on her pay from the salon, a fact that gulled Carol, she started to give Wendy bonuses in the form of cash kept in the filing cabinet, that money wasn't any of the Rev's business. Wendy had to get home, dinner was served at six o'clock every night without exception, it was an inexcusable sin not to be present when the Rev. Leroy Whitfield entered the room and took his place at the head of the table.

August 11th, 1980, Sueme's freedom:

The wheels of the government turn slowly, especially in a case as sensitive as the case of Sueme, the girl who had been with Margret for a month. Margret was becoming very attached to the girl, as was the whole staff, even the stern cook. Once when Margret was within earshot, she heard the cook howling with laughter as her big belly shock. Sueme was making impressions of famous movie stars. Margret received weekly reports from a physician, the initial report showed signs of dehydration, fatigue, starvation, and significant signs of sexual abuse. The latest report received showed the child was recovering, she gained ten pounds, her bruising and lacerations healed, the sexual abuse was healing but would take more time. A psychiatrist also saw Sueme on a weekly basis. The current report stated the girl felt safe with Margret and her mental state was stable, but her next placement would be critical in her overall ability to recover. The tutor reported to Margret daily, he was pleased with Sueme's progress, she was assessed to be reading on grade level, she was mastering the English language. If the Army could confirm Sueme's father was an American

Soldier, dead or alive, she would be going stateside, either to reside with his family or would be placed in a school for Veteran Children, she would be classified as a ward of the US government.

A corporal taught Sueme how to play chess; after she learned the game, her strategic moves would make a general proud, she loved the old piano in the library, simple tunes could be heard, the whole staff was charmed by a little girl.

Margret's motives were selfish, if the Army couldn't substantiate Sueme's claims, she was going to apply to adopt the child. As each day passed without notification from the Army, Margret's odds increased, but she knew the adoption would be unfair to Sueme. Margret was an Army brat, about every three years, her father would be reassigned, she didn't have a childhood friend, and she never had a town anywhere the family called home. Margret knew in her heart what was best for the child, but she also knew in her heart she loved the little girl who came to her with such a will to survive.

The report had arrived that morning and was on Margret's desk unopened after lunch the moment Margret dreaded finally became inevitable, she began to read the report. Margret hadn't cried since her days in the MASH unit, a daily influx of young soldiers wounded or DOA, and always more to come, but now, as she read and reread the findings she started to sob. An American soldier had been located, and Sueme would be leaving immediately, it was up to Margret to inform the staff, Sueme had given a person here something to remember, and it would take a long time to forget the little girl. Margret remembered Sueme's arrival and looking into a dirty tear-streaked face and the horrific story she had to tell. Margret put her selfish thoughts aside and hoped Sueme would have a hometown, friends, and a family to love and have the love returned.

Margret wrote a personal letter to accompany the files from the Army, which would be given to the family, asking to please keep her informed on Sueme. Upon completing the letter, Margret put her head on her desk and wept.

Tuesday August 12th, 1980

The Permanent Solution Salon was busy, but not as busy as the wagging tongues of the patrons; speculation and curiosity were running rampant in the small community concerning the William Westerkamp family. The newly appointed principal and his family were formally introduced tonight at the Coates County School Board meeting. Carol and Wendy listened to all the tidbits of gossip about the new family. Some patrons had brief encounters with family members while shopping at the IGA market or while transacting business at the bank. The conversation was mostly focused on the son, from what Wendy could gather the boy was a sight to behold, she would have the chance to find out, she had volunteered to help serve the buffet-style dinner prepared by the ladies of the cafeteria. Wendy liked being helpful, for the past three years, she had maintained the supply closet at school and had been approved to continue her job during her senior year, helping with the dinner was another way for her to avoid her home life with her father.

Buzz was in his office bright and early on Tuesday, he had a report to fill out about a break-in at Dolly and Mac's small general store. Dolly and Mac were both in their eighties, the sweetest people in the county, willing to give anyone the shirt off their back, now they were victims of a burglary. Mac called Buzz on Monday, August 11th, after returning from a trip to visit relatives to find the store door had been pried open, the cash in the register was gone, amounting to one hundred twenty-five dollars and some change, along with some snack foods. Buzz was angry, Dolly and Mac would give money, loan money, and share everything they had, it was sad that someone thought taking from these two generous people was a better idea. Buzz had gone to investigate, the lock on the door was very old, and prying the door was hardly necessary. The store was attached to the house, Buzz went to the hardware store and replaced both the lock on the store and the lock in the door of their residency. Dolly was more upset than Mac, she told Buzz for the longest time, they didn't lock their doors, and she wondered what was happening to the town of Coatesville. Buzz was wondering the same thing. Buzz asked Dolly and Mac to keep the incident to themselves, the thoughts Buzz had were grim. The only difference in Coatesville was the arrival of the Westerkamp family. The peeking tom issue had started before the arrival of the new residents, but the dead duck at the lake with a broken neck hanging on a fence post, and now this robbery was a little more than suspicious. Buzz and Betsy were going to attend the school board meeting, he was debating on wearing his uniform, not to intimidate but to make his presentence known. Buzz would pay strict attention to the young Mr. Westerkamp; maybe criminal activity was acceptable in Boston, but not in the county where he was the acting sheriff.

Evonne spent most of the day setting up the cafeteria for the dinner meeting, the head table would seat the members of the school board and the guests of honor, the new principal, and his family. Three large, beautiful bouquets were placed on the head table, the buffet tables were placed close to the kitchen, and a podium was centered at the front. Evonne could smell the aroma coming from the kitchen, the menu was fried chicken, scalloped potatoes, baked corn, coleslaw, and dinner rolls, a variety of cookies with coffee would be served for dessert.

Parents and concerned citizens started to arrive at six thirty. Seventy-five people were in attendance, the most in the history of a Coates County school board meeting. Buzz and Betsy grabbed a seat with Evonne and Brant Miller, Ty had to sit at the head table with the other board members, and Buzz had decided to wear his uniform, which didn't seem strange to anyone. At seven o'clock, the Westerkamp's arrived and were directed to the head table. Everyone settled in awaiting the start of the meeting. Mr. Stevens called the meeting to order, he addressed the crowd thanking them for a large turnout, he turned his attention to the guests, informing them a dinner had been prepared in their honor and was ready to be served. A line formed to be served from the buffet, with the guests being first, Wendy was serving the scalloped potatoes when she came face to face with Derek Westerkamp, she was stunned. When the dinner was finished, the dishes were cleared, while large trays with a variety of cookies and coffee were served, it was eight o'clock when Mr. Stevens took the podium and introduced Mr. William Westerkamp and family to the assembly. Anyone familiar with the military could tell instantly Mr. Westerkamp was a former soldier, his gait had a purpose, his stance was stern and erect, his speech was direct and decisive, a deep baritone voice with a distinctive Boston drawl. He thanked the board members for the opportunity awarded to him as the principal of the Coates County School District, he remarked about the delicious dinner served and complimented the kitchen staff, speaking to the large group of parents attending, he hoped their support would continue, working together to provide the best possible education for their children. William Westerkamp was six feet tall, thinning sandy colored hair, his complexion was rough and ruddy, with blue eyes and a nice warm smile. His wife was Sophia, he had met her while stationed in Spain, her hair was very dark with strands of gray, her facial features were sharp with deep olive skin, and she carried herself with dignity and grace. The biggest focus for most of the evening was Derek Westerkamp, he seemed to be a male model, a poster image for an Ivy League college teenage idol, his hair was lush and glossy the color of a raven, his complexion was deep olive, and his eyes were a crystal-clear blue, set in a face that could be mistaken for a Greek God. The navy blue blazer he wore looked tailored just for him, he wore a pale blue shirt with a stand-up collar and gray slacks with highly polished loafers. The only similarities between father and son were the blue eyes and the deep baritone voice with a heavy Boston drawl.

The speech Mr. Westerkamp delivered touched briefly on his military career, he had traveled throughout the world, he was trilingual, speaking Spanish and Italian, his passion was history and geography. He indicated he would like to introduce a Spanish course for any high school student, he was prepared to teach the class, he admitted physical education was of great importance to him. In conclusion to his speech, he thanked everyone for the warm welcome, and he hoped his family could make a positive contribution to the community and the school district. The assembly responded with a generous round of applause. Gus snapped a picture of Mr. Westerkamp standing behind his wife and son seated at the table, the photo would appear in Saturday's Coatesville Courier. Little did anyone know that picture would have significant importance in the fall of 1980 to solve a murder.

Buzz went back to his office to complete his report of the robbery that had taken place, he usually trusted his first impressions, but there was something that bothered him about the Westerkamp kid, he seemed too smooth, almost to the point of being smug, the performance Buzz witnessed at the school board meeting had his BS meter registering a ten.

Thursday, August 14th, 1980

Jack Furry was ready to make his move. The trucking company he planned on starting in Coates County was coming together. Every dime he had made while working the pipeline was gaining interest in the bank. Jack's plans were aggressive, he needed more financing, his account was sizeable but wouldn't be enough to cover land, construction and start-up costs, he called Brant Miller. The McKinny farm had several acres of untillable land, and Jack hoped Brant would sell him a portion of the land and invest in his company. Brant was a smart businessman, the deal would be a win-win situation, he would profit from the sale of useless land, and be invested in a profitable business while cutting his costs for shipping. Jack met with Brant and presented his proposal, Brant was very interested that a local trucking company would be beneficial, not only to the farmers but businesses like the feed and grain mill, Jack would get the land and the financial support he needed. A deal was struck between Jack Furry and Brant Miller, "The Blackjack" Tucking Company, with a tag line, "it's no gamble" would be a reality.

Jack's personal life was taking shape as well, he was becoming very fond of Nan, and at the diner, he still had every letter and photo Ruby had sent him, while he still loved Ruby, he couldn't continue to live in the past, it was time for a future. The age difference between Jack and Nan was ten years, that fact didn't bother either of them. Nan wasn't hard to look at, her face was cute with a youthful glow, she was soft-spoken and never did anything to earn the reputation she had with a group of "Holier than Thou" women the area. As a young girl the only source of emotional support Carol had was her mother, and she had depended on Ruby in his absence, Jack wasn't sure how Carol would react to his relationship with Nan, it was a conversation that was unavoidable. Jack loved Carol more than anything in the world; they were building a good father-daughter rapport, but he wasn't willing to ask Nan to settle for a clandestine romance, he respected her too much for that.

Today was a big day for Evonne, she was due at the bank at ten o'clock for the settlement on the house on Beyers Avenue she bought from an estate sale. There was a lot of work to be completed before she could occupy the house, she had a carpenter, a plumber, and a painter ready to restore the dwelling. The only piece of furniture she wanted from Clark was the rocking chair her dad had made for the nursery. He could do everything else, she wondered how Clark would react to that. Gossip in town was Clark was dating a young blonde woman, the word was she had practically moved into the house on Ellis Avenue, the same house Evonne had resided in as Clark's wife two weeks ago, his grief over Evonne leaving must have been short-lived. Evonne hoped they would be very happy together, she wondered how long the young woman would stay after Clark's money ran out. After the transaction at the bank, Evonne was going to see a lawyer to file divorce papers, she considered herself a lucky girl, the purchase a home, while getting rid of an abusive albatross all in one day.

The weather had turned nasty, a typical summer thunderstorm was passing over, causing heavy rain and strong wind gusts, Ty found shelter in the barn. The things Ty took for granted in her youth had become so vivid and alive: the wildflowers in the meadows, the smell of fresh-cut hay, and the beauty of the gentle rolling hills, the house was even different. Sadness replaced love, laughter, and a promise for the future. After a long day of work, the front porch became a haven for Ty, Brant, and her father-in-law, sharing a glass of iced tea while the shadows grew longer and darkness replaced the daylight.

Ty had every reason to be hopeful, her first menstrual period since her marriage was late, could it be possible she and Brant had already conceived, and she was carrying Brant's baby. Today had brought a host of problems: a large tractor had broken an axle, the vet was there for a cow about to give birth, and one of the exhaust fans in the barn stopped working. There were phones in every building all connected to the house, when the phone in the barn started to ring Ty wondered what else could go wrong, she was about to find out. The call was from Rosa, the housekeeper. Her voice was excited, speaking in a mixture of her native Spanish and some English, Ty caught a phrase about two men who were at the house and wanted to speak to her. Ty entered the back door, Rosa rushed to her and gestured by shrugging her shoulders and pointing to the family room. Ty went to see what all the ado was about.

Two men confronted her, and both were in full-dress Army uniforms. Both men stood upon her arrival, "Mrs Tyler Summers" was the greeting, it had been so long since Ty had even thought about her former married name, she fumbled for an answer. Ty finally found her voice, what she said was sharp and to the point, "Yes, I was married to Andrew Summers about thirteen years ago until he got drafted into the Army and lost his life in Vietnam, as far as I know I have claimed all his possessions along with his body. I can't think of any possible reason you would need to speak to me, I have moved on with my life and have no intention or desire to dredge up old and bitter memories." Ty animosity was evident for the war, and the two men now intruding in her new life, the two men seemed unruffled by Ty's rebuff and introduced themselves as Captain Reynolds and Captain Ramsey. Captain Reynolds did most of the talking, there was a serious issue they needed to discuss with her, he asked Ty if they could take a seat. Ty gestured toward a sofa, she took the sofa across from the men, separated by a coffee table, she wanted to get the issue settled and have these men gone.

After the men were seated, Captain Ramsey placed a briefcase over his knees, and pulled out a file along with a picture which he laid on the coffee table in front of Ty, "is this a picture of your deceased husband, Andrew Summers?" Ty studied the picture, she saw a young man with no shirt, wearing a pair of fatigues, with his foot propped on a rock and a riffle across his leg, but there was no doubt it was Andy.

Andy Summers came to work on the McKinny farm when Ty was nineteen years old, she was at the height of an over barring, self-indulging, spoiled brat era. Her father couldn't keep stable hands, he was fed up with her attitude and let Ty know if she didn't stop treating the farm help so poorly, she would be left to do the stable work herself if she wanted to keep horses on the farm. Ty thought her father was joking until she met Andy, while riding one day, she approached the stable when a young man stepped out in front of her and caused her horse to rear, she maintained control and brought the horse to a halt. Ty was furious and full of rage when she slid off her horse and confronted the man, and she was even more exasperated when he seemed to be unfazed by the incident. She confronted Andy with full raft and a sense of entitlement, demanding an answer to why he scared her horse, standing face to face with the man she wanted to know why he was skulking around the stable. Andy didn't answer at once, he pulled his tee shirt off, dried his face and tied the shirt around his waist. Ty noticed he was perspiring, mixing with the oils from his body, showing a very tanned and well-developed chest, she tried not to show her loss of composure at the sight of the stranger standing before her as she continued her tyrant. Ty demanded he tell her who he was, his reply was slow and mocking, "I'm Andy Summers, your dad hired me as a trainer-stable hand." "Then why aren't you working instead of standing around and scaring my horse," Ty said in response. "I'm on a break, and I didn't scare your horse, you scared your horse by pulling up too hard on the reins." She tossed the reins to Andy and ordered him to cool the horse down and give him water, much to Ty's surprise, Andy told her, "You rode the horse, you cool it down, your father has already given me a list of work for the day." Ty was out of control with anger and asked him if he knew who he was talking to, Andy replied in a voice filled with humor said, "no, I don't think I have had the pleasure of making your acquaintance." Ty stomped around

Andy and took the horse to his stall while Andy followed, he stood in the doorway and kept a steady gaze on her, which made her nervous for some reason, she told him to put his shirt on because he was sweaty and stinking. "Oh, I beg your pardon, Miss, the sweat and stink result from hard work. Maybe you should try it sometime, it's good for the soul", Andy said evenly. Ty told him to do as he was told, and she started to the stable door in a huff, just as she reached the door, she heard Andy say, "Woo Wee, what a bitch".

By the time Ty entered the kitchen, she was ready to confront her father about the insubordinate, pompous ass he had hired as a stable hand, her father was in the kitchen making a sandwich, and Ty seized the opportunity to demand Andy's dismissal. Sam was growing weary of Ty's childish demanding behavior; in the past year, he had hired three stable hands, and they had all quit even with the money he paid in wages. Sam made it clear to Ty that Andy was staying, and she better make the best of the arrangement because if he quit, she would be left to work in the stable. Ty was shocked and stormed to her bedroom, slamming the door, she sat in front of her mirror and realized her face was flushed, but she wasn't sure if the flushing was from anger. Ty had never met anyone like Andy, she couldn't help but think of his well-built body and commanding nature, for no one ever dealt with her in such a manner.

Over the next several days, Ty didn't see Andy and she wondered if she had quit too. One morning, while getting her mount ready for a ride, Andy appeared in the stall doorway, and the sight of him caused Ty to jump. "A little skittish this morning," Andy asked as he leaned against the stall door. "Do you make a habit of scaring the horses?" asks Ty trying to maintain her composure. "I wasn't talking about the horse," and he added with a slow smile while staring into Ty's eyes, "Do you know why your father hired me, I'm good at breaking stubborn fillies."

Ty was ready to be broken; the couple spent every free moment with each other, and then Andy got a letter with the heading, GREETING FROM THE PRESIDENT, it was his draft notice. Ty and Andy eloped before he was scheduled to leave for boot camp, after six weeks of basic training, he was furloughed for two weeks spent as the couple's honeymoon. Ty never saw Andy alive again, instead, she had to wait while an Army transport plane unloaded the coffin, barring Andy's body, Andy Summers was the only man in Coates County to lose his life in Vietnam. Ty was bitter for a long time, but now she had found her true love, Brant, and she didn't want to deal with the past.

The past had come to visit, dumped into Ty's lap, and there was an unsettling feeling in the pit of her stomach, it was a long time before Ty spoke, and in an almost inaudible voice, she verified it was Andy in the picture.

"We are from the Army Personnel Office in Washington D.C., and we have a matter of great importance to speak with you about," said Capt. Ramsey. Capt. Reynolds pulled out another photo of Andy, a military picture with his identification. "Would you please verify the photo and the facts in his file?" Ty was trying to make sense of the questioning and needed answers, this was a part of her life she left behind, and she wasn't sure if Brant knew of her marriage to Andy. Ty read over the dates, times, and places, and verified the information as being true. The next statement from Capt. Ramsey left Ty stunned and cold inside, "We have reason to believe your husband, Andrew Summers, while in Vietnam sponsored as a child."

Ty sat in stunned silence, just this morning, her life was perfect, she was married to a man she loved more than anything in the world and was hoping to start a family of her own. When Ty recovered from her shock, she asked the obvious question, "What brought the Army to the conclusion that my late husband was responsible for a child while in Vietnam?" Reynolds responded, "The child is a girl, she is thirteen years old, her name is Sueme. The girl came to the Army seeking refuge from two abusive uncles who had taken custody of the child after her mother died over a year ago. In her possession was a small handbag with a few coins, a pill, and a picture of a soldier her mother claimed was the girl's American father." Ty was outraged, a picture didn't prove the child belonged to her late husband, Capt. Ramsey picked up the conversation, "the Army has done extensive research on the matter, the location is right, your late husband was stationed in that area at the time of the girl's birth, his blood type is the same as the girl's blood type." Ty's response was tight, "Andy's blood type was O positive, there are millions of men in the world with that blood type, I suppose the child wants to come to the United States." "The girl is already in the United States. She is now a ward of the Army. Before we place the child in a Veterans home for Children, the Army wanted to be sure every possible avenue was explored for the next of kin," the Capt. answered. Capt. Reynolds placed the girl's only possessions with her upon meeting Major Margret Starr, on the coffee table, Ty stared at a photo, a few coins and a pill, but there wasn't any doubt it was a picture of Andy.

Ty's emotions were tumbling over and over in her mind, she was hurt that Andy was in Vietnam for such a short period before he sought the company of another woman. Ty and Andy were only married two weeks before he was shipped out, if the girl was thirteen, he would have been with the child's mother almost from the start. Andy's indiscretions were now dropped in her lap, Ty was so upset she blurted out, "What does all of this have to do with me, I am not to blame for my late husband's actions, the child is not blood kin. I understand the picture but what are the coins and the pill, is the child sick." "No, madam, the child claims she earned the coins before she left her uncle's home, and the pill is Cyanide," replied Ramsey.

"CYANIDE," Ty's voice heightened a couple of octaves, "why would a thirteen-year-old girl have a cyanide pill?" Capt. Ramsey responded, "I have questioned the child, I have every reason to believe what she told me. Her mother gave her the pill, it was unknown to the South Vietnamese people the treatment or punishment they might endure after the American Troops left the area. Her mother instructed the girl to have control of the terms and time of her death and not to leave that decision to the enemy. The child was fully prepared to take the pill if she was captured and returned to her uncles's custody." He pulled out a large folder and placed it on the table in front of Ty, "I will leave this report with you, if you decide to take the child the report will remain with you, if not, the report will be sealed until the child is eighteen. Here is my number and extension, please let me know your decision as soon as possible, you have been investigated by the Army and have been approved for sponsorship, it is important to get the child settled somewhere and get her in school. The report must be signed by you whatever way you decide." The two men stood and bid Ty a farewell, and they were gone.

Ty picked up the report and started to read; it read like a horror story, some words and phrases jumped out at her, starvation, day slavery, prostitution, dehydration, cyanide, and sexual abuse. It was tough reading and even harder to believe that a young child had to endure such an existence. Ty felt shame, her childhood was pampered, self-indulged, and spoiled rotten, while this girl had to escape a life of horror. Tears filled Ty's eyes, she cried for the girl, for the betrayal she felt for Andy, and for the fact she would have to tell Brant about her past.

Brant couldn't find Ty anywhere; he called the house, and Rose told him two men were there to visit Ty, leaving her in a terrible emotional state. Brant found Ty in the family room sobbing, not knowing what the problem was, he took the sofa facing Ty, she looked at him with swollen eyes and said I'm so sorry. The story tumbled out, she had eloped early in her life with Andy, he had died in the war, she didn't think about that part of her life until today and the reason the two Army officers had paid their visit. Brant listened, he told Ty he knew she had eloped, and at the time he wanted to beat her ass, he thought Andy was a very good trainer and a hard worker, but he had the worst reputation in a tri-county area, he was a womanizer and would have never been faithful to her as a husband. Ty was so relieved she started to babble, she told him about the child, and left Brant to read the report, he was shocked and angry. Ty admitted she wasn't sure she could take a child who was a source of her betrayal and not show her bitterness to the child. Brant told Ty to leave Andy out of the equation, whether he was the father or not, with all you have to offer. Would you open your heart and provide a home for a child who desperately needed safety and security, not to mention love? The answer was so simple, she looked at Brant and knew why she loved him, Ty and Brant were going to have a child sooner than they thought.

Sunday August 17th, 1980

Wendy, the daughter of the "do as I say, not as I do" preacher.

Wendy vowed to be an exception to the rule of Coatesville; most residents remained generation after generation, but she had her sights set on college and escaping her overbearing father. The Rev. Leroy Whitfield was a self-serving, arrogant, pompous ass, a man by profession who should have been a loving husband and father. Instead, Wendy was the product of a loveless marriage; she often wondered how she was ever conceived. Her mother (Betty) was a helpless, pitiful, unloved woman who was directly under the thumb of her husband; she wore plain dark-colored dresses, mid-calf length, black leather shoes that could only be described as ugly, no make-up, and her hair was pulled back so tight her eyebrows appeared to be arched. The Rev's attire was a sharp contrast: very expensive suits, stiff starched white shirts, silk ties with hankies to match, and black slip-on loafers with tassels, which was made possible by the tithing provided by the hard-working people of Coatesville.

Shame was what Wendy felt concerning the tactics her father used to abscond money from the honest, hard-working people of the county; the Rev. showed little remorse for the quality of life of his parishioners. The only quality of life he showed any concern for was his own life. One of his favorite ploys was a classic: while preaching from the pulpit, he would grow silent, raise his bible high in the air, and appear to be in a trance. Five or more minutes would pass without a word from the Rev., he would suddenly start to speak in tongues, leaving the whole congregation in complete awe. The so-called trance would end, and the Rev. would tell the congregation he had a vision from God, the visions were often in the form of fundraisers, which meant extra tithing was expected. The more money the Rev. deemed necessary, the longer the trance, and the louder the speaking in tongues became, the whole performance was likened to a carnival sideshow, or a bad movie about a flim-flam evangelist. Amazingly the congregation would open their wallets and the tithing in the coffer would increase, which was the only thing that ever made Rev. Leroy Whitfield happy.

The Rev Leroy never failed to use his pulpit to promote male superiority, he belittled women for their wanton behavior and disobedient, showing his total disrespect to the female gender. He cited quotes from the Bible about braided hair and costly array, he indicated women alone were responsible for the woes of the world throughout the ages, including the Original Sin. One word the Rev. would use loudly and frequently concerning women was Whore, society has no place for a whore, they should fall on their knees and beg God to cleanse their souls of their sins, a woman was to be chosen by one man, being responsible for satisfying his wants and needs. The Rev. could rail on for hours about the qualities a good Christian woman should possess, meekness, humbleness, submissiveness to her husband, and purity of mind, in other words, under a male's thumb. One of the most unforgivable sins a woman could commit was wearing white shoes on Sunday to church, Wendy's mother was not allowed to own a pair of white shoes. Some of the residents didn't attend the church in Coatesville, they would travel to another county, while some considered the Rev. Leroy radical, others like Carol, thought he was nuts.

The church was located on Walnut Ave, the home of the Whitfields abutted the church, Wendy's bedroom was on the second-floor loaf area, it was her escape haven from her father. The bedroom windows provided Wendy a view of the church courtyard, and the old cemetery was surrounded by wrought iron fence, which was the resting place for many generations of residents, dating the post- civil war era. Wendy hated Sundays, part of her chores each week was to prepare the church for morning services, dust the pews, and make sure the hymnals were in their proper place. August was humid, with only hot air to ventilate the musky, dank aroma of the church, Wendy would coat her nostrils with Vick's vapor rub to avoid the smell. The church was plainly adorned, with no flowers, no musical accompaniment for the hymns, and no window coverings, the pulpit was placed on a raised platform with a single straight-backed chair for Betty. The old carpet was thread barren, and the paint had yellowed over the years and started cracking and peeling. Behind the pulpit was a single large wooden cross, the only other item on the rear wall was a sign with replaceable numbers to indicate the past week's attendance and the tithing from the prior week. Services started promptly at nine o'clock, Wendy's usual seat was the front row, outer edge; she liked to sit in the corner of the pew, it enabled her to look at the faces of the congregation and watch the expression change.

Wendy became aware that it was eight-forty-five, and she had to finish her chores and return the cleaning supplies to her father's office. The Rev's office was a testimony to his sense of self-worth; the windows had slatted blinds, and one had a large air conditioning unit, which cooled the office very nicely, even on the hottest days. The carpet was far from being thread barren, the bookcases were highly polished along with the desk and swivel chair. The walls were freshly painted and covered with dozens of pictures, all showing the Rev. and someone he deemed important, with each new photo he would share the significance of the relationship to the congregation. The photos missing from his Wide Wall of Fame were pictures of his wife and daughter. Wendy has a burning desire to become more important than the people he placed above her mother and herself. The photos cause a bitter bile to rise in Wendy's throat, but she soon forgets about her disgust when she notices a notebook lying on her father's desk. The notebook was the same as the journal she wrote all her thoughts, things she couldn't tell anyone, but writing them in her book, it was as good as confiding her thoughts to someone. The Rev. had a habit of snooping, she remembered a time when he found a tube of lipstick in her purse, she tried to explain, but it was no use, he grabbed her by the hair and painted her entire face with the lipstick, he told her if she wanted to look like a Whore, he would help her out. Now she was wondering if he had been rifling through her bedroom and found her journal. Her legs turned to rubber and her hands were shaking as she rounded the desk to look closer. Suddenly, the room was so hot Wendy thought she was suffocating; she grabbed the book and almost tore the cover off apprehension of what she might discover. The relief was instant when she saw what looked to be a list of expenses, Wendy's curiosity got the better of her judgment, she started to read. Listed on the second page was a notation that completely puzzled her, there was the word "Winter" with a star beside the entry and the cost of fifty dollars. Wendy didn't have a clue what that expense was, but she stored the information in her mind, and would later try to do more investigating, but it was time to take her place in the front row of the church.

The summer season always brought a decline in church attendance, which meant the coffers would diminish, a great concern to the Rev. The sermon started at nine o'clock as usual, Wendy wondered what new ploy her father would employ to increase the offering, she got a vision of her father standing on the platform handling snakes, she had to maintain a straight face at that thought. Thankfully, her father's droning was over, the collection plates were passed, and the final hymn was announced, it was "How Great Thou Are", Wendy knew it was to be a tribute to her father.

Wendy was able to escape to the sanity of her bedroom, she was anxious to retrieve her journal and make sure it hadn't been tampered with. She made a mental note to take her notebook to Carol's salon for safekeeping.

Wendy was looking forward to her senior year of high school, she had three close friends she didn't see much of over the summer: Missy Evans and the Anderson Twins, Cal, and Cliff. The Spanish class Mr. Westerkamp talked about at the school board meeting was of interest to Wendy, so was the son of the new principal, Derek Westerkamp. Gus Johnson printed the picture of the Westerkamp taken at the school board meeting. Derek made quite an impression on the teen girls in the area, and he became a permanent fixture at the Dairy Queen, a favorite hang-out. The Anderson twins were very special to Wendy, they had been friends since grade school. They attended dances together, but she never had deep feelings for either Cal or Cliff, but both boys fiercely protected her.

Wendy applied to three different colleges, she didn't care which one accepted her, she just wanted to put as much distance between her father and herself, the only guilt she felt was leaving her mother with no joy left in her life. Wendy loved her mother, she enjoyed Wednesdays alone with her; the Rev. was away from the house every Wednesday to attend a church council meeting held in Center County. Together they would pig out on everything that was otherwise forbidden in the Whitfield house, with Wendy's earnings she was able to treat her mother.

Every week's meals were the same, the Rev. kept a tight rein on the budget for groceries, and Sunday evening was the standard fired chicken, Wendy knew she would have to leave the peace and quiet of her loft to help her mother in the kitchen. Betty Whitfield's face brightened when Wendy entered the kitchen, it was difficult for Wendy to witness what her mother had become, little more than a servant to a man who showed contempt for her efforts. The Rev. took his seat at the head of the table at exactly six o'clock, the conversation was unnecessary, he never sought his wife's opinion, Betty wasn't an equal partner or life mate, just a subordinate. Wendy didn't even bother to engage in any communication with her father, she had given up on seeking his approval, trying for years to gain his love, only to be rebuffed. She was starting to see the fine line between love and hate. The Rev. said the prayer at the table every meal, he thanked God but never thanked his wife and daughter for the part they played in the meal being put on the table at exactly six o'clock per his demand. When the Rev. finished his last bite, he silently left the kitchen, Wendy and her mother were left alone to carry on a conversation, while Betty was relieved another meal was finished, Wendy wanted to scream at her father and slap his face. Wendy knew she could love; she now realized her hatred could be as strong.

Thursday August 28th, 1980

Sueme; Home on the range:

Sueme was due to arrive at eleven o'clock, accompanied by Capt. Ramsey, since Ty's discovery of the child's existence, her acceptance of the facts, and Brant's wisdom concerning the past, Ty was ready to open her home and heart to this girl regardless of her parentage. Ty went into full decorator mode, her old childhood bedroom was transformed, and all the trophies, ribbons and awards were packed in boxes. It was amazing all the things she used to covet were also a part of the past she wanted to bury. The bedroom was painted pale pink, the trophy case was replaced with bookshelves filled with books, puzzles, and games. Ty had opted for white furniture, two dressers, a vanity with a large mirror, the thick, lush bed's quilt and shams were pink and white checked, a small white piano was placed between two windows. Ty had a comb and brush set with pearl handles her parents bought her for her eleventh birthday, she put on the vanity along with a manicure set and plenty of youthful scents of perfume, the bathroom was loaded with soaps, lotions, toothbrush, and paste. Ty assessed the bedroom, trying to imagine what a thirteen-year-old girl might like, she rearranged the furniture twice, and changed her mind about the color of the throw rugs; now, just hours before Sueme's arrival, she was finally satisfied with the finished look.

Ty and Brant opened the door and came face to face with Sueme; Ty noticed the child moved closer to Capt. Ramsey when confronted by two strangers. The girl was taller than Ty expected, her face was cute with lingering signs of childhood. Ty couldn't say by looking at Sueme if Andy was her father, but she knew the child had a lot of American blood mixed with her Asian heritage. Ty led the way down the long hall to the great room, Sueme almost fell down the two stairs leading into the room, she was staring at the room in awe. The room was huge, two large sofas were in the center with a long coffee table separating the two, and a massive stone fireplace covered one wall, erected with some of the original stones from Harrison McKinny's first house. An open staircase led to the loft area, the back wall was glass windows raising two stories, providing a panoramic view of the farm. Sueme looked at Capt. Ramsey for directions, he indicated to her a seat on one of the sofas, the Capt. told Ty he needed to speak to her alone. Brant sat across from Sueme and tried to engage her in conversation while Ty and the Capt. went to the office; the Capt. told Ty, "Sueme hadn't quit grasping the reality of freedom, she will always ask for permission to do everything, including using the bathroom, she won't eat in less she is told, and is very apprehensive when a stranger is introduced into her life". Capt. Ramsey continued "in time she will become comfortable, she is very open, witty, and intelligent. The file containing Sueme's information consisted of a current report from an

Army psychiatrist, her updated medical status, and a hand-written letter from Major Margret Starr, which was signed by Capt. Ramsey, Sueme was released into the custody of Ty Miller. Ty noticed the birth certificate listed Andrew Summers as the father, reading that information didn't faze Ty, from now on, the child was going to be Sueme Miller, daughter of Tyler and Brant Miller.

Ty and Capt. Ramsey returned to the great room to find Brant engaged in a one-way conversation with Sueme about the horses on the farm, her body language told Ty the girl had started to relax, she wasn't sitting on the edge of the seat as if she might have to escape at any moment. The Capt. was ready to leave, Sueme went to the Capt., hugged him, and thanked him for all he had done for her. For an instant, Ty saw the stoic military appearance disappear; Capt. Ramsey recovered quickly and was gone.

Ty wanted to get the child settled as soon as possible, so she showed her around the house, introduced her to Rosa, and her new bedroom was the last, Brant picked up the lone suitcase and the trio went upstairs to the loft area. Sueme stopped at the landing, stood at the rail for a long time, and looked out at the farm, her eyes came to rest on the stallion roaming the corral. Ty guided Sueme down the hall to a door with "Sueme" written in script, encircled with delicate flowers, Ty opened the door and went and sat on the bed, hoping to gauge Sueme's reaction, the look on Sueme's face broke Ty's heart, it was like a poor orphan child peering into the window of a fancy toy store. Ty cranked the music box set on a dresser, Sueme watched as the ballerina spun around while the music played, she ran her fingers over the fine wood of the furniture. She stared at the bookcase and tilted her head as if she were trying to read the titles on the book's spine, her attention turned to the games and puzzles, she pulled a game off the shelf and examined it, wondering if it was real. The big white teddy bear on the bed was a gift from Evonne, it was originally the bear in Evonne's never-to-be-used nursery, it caught Sueme's eye, she patted the furry stuffed toy, and she poked her fingers in the quilt and pillow shams to see if they were as soft as they looked. Ty had installed a white phone on the nightstand, Sueme lifted the receiver and listened to the dial tone, she walked to a window and stared at another beautiful view of the farm. The piano was sitting between the windows,

Sueme lightly touched a few of the keys, and everything seemed real, much to her amazement. Sueme's tour ended at the vanity. She sat down and stared in the mirror, expecting an image of another girl, the girl who truly occupied this room, and she was just dreaming. Sueme remembered the old, filthy worn mattress she shared with bugs and every man in the village, it seemed a world away and an eon of time ago, the mirror showed Ty standing behind her, she could only hope this was all real. Sueme said to Ty, in a voice that was almost a whisper, "Miss Ty, is this all for me?" Ty stood behind Sueme while they looked at each other in the mirror, "Yes, this is all for you."

Rosa appeared in the doorway and announced that lunch was ready, when Sueme was leaving her new bedroom, she turned and gave a final look before closing the door carefully. Brant and Ty agreed on a couple of things concerning Sueme's early days with her new family, first to have her homeschooled for a year to ensure she was on a proper grade level to enter a public school, and not to force her into conversation. The family went to the casual dining area in the kitchen, lunches were mostly soup and sandwiches, Bill, Brant's father, always came in from his chores for lunch. Ty watched as Bill appeared at the table, she was afraid Sueme would go completely silent, but much to Ty's surprise, the girl responded to Bill's greeting with "Hi, my name is Sueme and added in the same breath, Mr. Brant. When can I see the horses"? Ty and Brant looked at each other, smiled and winked, the first steps of Sueme's new life were taking place.

7:00 pm.

Mr. Westerkamp called a staff meeting to discuss the upcoming school year; the meeting was to start at seven o'clock in the cafeteria, and all Coates County school system employees were to be in attendance. When Evonne arrived, the atmosphere was light and jovial, Mr. Westerkamp was circulating throughout the room, learning names and positions. A portable chalkboard was placed at the front of the room; Evonne noticed Mr. Westerkamp didn't have a single reference note as he started his address to the staff. The first topic was his visions, the school board had approved a Spanish class, a maximum of fifteen students would be accepted, and physical education was the next point; each child, grades one through six, will have two recess periods per day, the high school students will have three gym classes per week. School hours were the next point, the final bell would ring at three fifteen, and all students would be gone from the building by three thirty, in less they were involved in an after-school activity. Mr. Westerkamp directed his next remarks to the janitors, they were to have their work completed by four fifteen and exit the building no later than four thirty, he continued, the supply room locks have been changed, only three keys to the new lock will be issued, the head janitor, Wendy Whitfield, and himself, all other keys were to be turned into the office as soon as possible. Evonne was starting to get an uneasy feeling, she tried to glance sideways to catch expressions on other faces. Mr. Westerkamp wasn't any easier on the teachers, they were to be gone from the building by four thirty, any teacher holding an after-school conference was to inform him of the time and date and the nature of the meeting.

There will be a new system of disciplinary measures in place for the new school year; Mr. Westerkamp flipped the chalkboard over to reveal a demerit system. One demerit will be issued for infractions like chewing gum, profanity, tardiness, or talking in class, with the accumulation of six demerits, a student is suspended for a day, non-physical confrontation would be a one-day instant suspension, and physical confrontations will be an instant three-day suspension. Evonne was stunned, she knew Mr. Westerkamp had a military background, but this was a school system, not a military academy.

Mr. Westerkamp continued; the first day of school will be Tuesday, September 2nd; all high school students will report to the cafeteria at eight o'clock, where I will explain the demerit system. A new alarm system has been installed on the exit doors of the building, after four thirty pm., the doors automatically lock when exiting, the only access to the building between the hours of four thirty pm. And seven o'clock the following day will be the main entrance. If there are any questions, I will remain here for a little while, the meeting is adjourned. The crowd started to disperse quickly, the whole evening had changed course, what started with happy chit-chat had turned to silent apprehension, Evonne was baffled, and by the expressions on the faces of her co-workers as she was leaving, "baffled" was the consensus.

Sunday August 31st, 1980

Wendy rose earlier than usual; dawn was just breaking. She was looking out her bedroom window at the church courtyard and old cemetery. Most of the headstones were over a hundred years old, weather-beaten granite markers with a name, birth date and date of death were the only reminders of the once-living soul buried deep in the earth. The cemetery always seemed sad to Wendy. Even on the sunniest days, she could envision groups of mourners saying a final prayer and weeping as the first shovel of dirt fell on the casket of a loved one and the long grieving process began. Wendy's whole image of the old graveyard, sadness, and grief had managed to ooze into the church and her home. Her father had stolen her mother's soul a long time ago, with each passing loveless year of marriage, another shovel of dirt buried her deeper into an empty, joyless existence. Wendy loved her mother and hoped one day she could show her a different world, but she was fearful her mother was already dead inside, resigning herself to her fate.

Wendy wasn't dreading today. Carol was having a picnic, and she was going to be attending after the morning church services, it was a chance to escape the confines of the house and her father. The church was stifling, the musty aromas hung in the air with no way to escape, the smell penetrated every corner of the old building. The office area was Wendy's focus, she wanted to see if the notebook she had discovered had any new entries, she leafed through the pages, and there, listed again was the word "Winter" with fifty dollars in the debt column. The notebook contained about six months of expenditures, Wendy examined the entire book, counting the number of times the word "Winter" appeared, the total was seven. Wendy replaced the book just as she had found it and took her place in the front row, the service was about to begin. The Rev. had been in a particularly bad mood lately, attendance was down, and the tithings reflected the low numbers. The Rev. Whitfield's mood was apparent in his extra-long sermon of hell, fire, and damnation, he badgered on about "fun" being a fool's folly and poor entertainment choices. From Wendy's vantage point in the front row, she saw sagging bodies and heads bowed in shame; she often wondered if anyone ever left the church with a spiritual lift, or did they feel as she did, no amount of effort would ever be favourable in the eyes of Rev.

Leroy Whitfield. The collection plates were passed, and a final hymn was sung, Wendy hurried to the house to change her clothing, she imagined her dresses always smelled like the dank, musty church. The Rev. didn't have any use for picnics, he didn't even attend the annual harvest celebration, he couldn't take the time to honour the hard work of the farmers of the county even though their tithes were a big part of church funding.

The picnic was perfect, it didn't take Wendy long to forget the morning service, her father's long sermon, or the dank smell of the church. The only memories Wendy had from her childhood that vaguely resembled a picnic was when a group of parishioners volunteered to do repairs and paint the church, Betty made them each a sandwich and a few chips for lunch. The Rev. paid strict attention to the amount of money for the extra expense added to the weekly grocery account. Betty served the lunch while the volunteers spread blankets in the old courtyard, that was the only recollection Wendy had of a gathering at the Whitfield Home.

The aroma from the grill loaded with hamburgers and hot dogs could be smelled a block away, a large, galvanized tub was full of ice and sodas, and two tables were placed under a large oak tree. Hoops and stakes were set for a game of croquet, and while Jack and Tom faced off in horseshoes, Wendy joined the women in the kitchen, putting the final touches on the side dishes. Jack invited Nan, who makes the best coleslaw in the county and brought a generous bowl to share, Tom hollered that the burgers and dogs were ready, everyone grabbed a paper plate and a chair on the lawn, Wendy was amazed by the ease of the conversation, it was very different than the silent meals at home. The fun lasted for hours, Jack and Wendy teamed together in a game of croquet against Carol and Tom, and elimination rounds were played in horseshoes until Jack was declared the champion. When the cake was served, Wendy felt a sense of sadness, the picnic was ending, she wished could remain stationary in time. The time had come, Wendy said her goodbye and started her walk home, with each step her spirits were sinking like the sun on the western horizon, and only darkness lay ahead.

As Wendy approached the house, she could hear her father's angry voice, she tried to enter the front door and go straight to her loft haven, but her father stopped her. Wendy was summoned to the kitchen, the Rev. was reaming Betty on the grocery budget, but he turned his full raft toward her when she entered the room. The picnic was the subject of the Rev's anger, Wendy had asked for permission to attend, but like everything else in her life the Rev. wasn't paying attention, he assumed the picnic was on Monday, Labor Day, and not Sunday. He told Wendy only a whore wears shorts, that her behaviour was a disgrace to his position in the county, and she was flaunting her flesh, Wendy could feel the tears welling up in her eyes. Betty Whitfield snapped her hand down on the table. She stood up and faced off with her husband, "That's enough. You have robbed me of many years, I will not allow you to rob Wendy of her youth" Betty had a fire in her voice. The Rev. was stunned momentarily but recovered quickly, "You both make me sick, stay out of my sight", and he stormed out of the house. Wendy had to escape, she went out the backdoor and started to run, she stumbled and fell, Nan also lived on Walnut Ave., at that moment, Jack's truck turned the corner bringing Nan home from the picnic. Wendy threw herself into Jack's arms and began to cry uncontrollably, he gently consoled her and wondered what had happened, just a few hours ago they were all having a wonderful day. Once in the house, Wendy recounted the scene with her father, Nan was tending to her scraped knee, by the time Wendy finished her story, Jack was ragging mad. Wendy asked Nan why her father hated her so much, Nan's reply was simple and quick, "I don't think your father is capable of love except for himself, I have lived on this street for many years, and in all that time your father has never had a pleasant word to say to me or about me, but that works both ways". Jack stood by and watched the anguish and hurt Wendy experienced at the hands of the Rev. Leroy Whitfield, at that moment Jack was thinking of revenge. Soon Jack was going to visit the Rev. for a man to man talk, if the Rev. thought Wendy caused him shame and compromised his position in the county, Jack was sure the information he had would destroy his position in the county.

Jack insisted on walking Wendy up the street to her house, she crept inside and up to her loft, her father probably didn't know she was gone. Sleep was eluding Wendy; she lay awake for a long time thinking about the fun day at the picnic and the nightmare that followed. Wendy adored Jack and wished she could select her family, Jack would be her grandfather, he showed her more compassion and love than she had ever felt from her father. A smile crossed Wendy's lips as she thought about her mother standing up to her father on her behalf, it worried Wendy about the price her mother might have to pay in the future for her disrespectful outburst. The new school was starting on Tuesday, and she turned her thoughts to her senior year and reconnecting with her friends.

The day was wonderful for the newly formed Miller family. Sueme was quickly adapting to her newfound freedom and family, she liked American food, the wide-open areas of the farm, and she loved her new grandfather, Bill. She called Bill "pap", if Bill was in the area, Sueme would be close by. She rode with Bill to check for broken fences and started wearing jeans and boots. The stable was a major interest for Sueme, Brant was teaching how to ride, but warned her of the hard work involved in riding and maintaining the stable. Sueme went about cleaning the stalls and grooming like she was an old hand. Bill lived on the west bank of the largest pond on the McKinny farm, it was a perfect setting for a cookout. An old pier on the lake provided a perfect spot for swimming, a paddle boat was docked at the pier and Sueme spent hours on the water, pedalling from one end of the big pond to the other. The cookout was simple, hotdogs on sticks over an open flame and s'mores, by evening Sueme was happy and exhausted. Ty was very happy, almost sure she was pregnant, with each passing day she became more hopeful the doctor would be able to confirm her thoughts as reality. Occasionally, Sueme would have an expression on her face that reminded her of Andy, but Ty wasn't sure if it was her imagination. There was a nagging feeling in the back of Ty's mind, Sueme seemed just a slight bit guarded with her. Ty wasn't jealous of the open loving relationship Sueme had with Brant and Bill, she wondered if she was expecting too much, or if Sueme longed for a father figure she never had to this point. Ty knew Sueme loved her, but she knew there was some reason Sueme wasn't quite as responsive to her, not surrendering her whole heart like she did with Brant and Bill.

Tuesday September 2nd, 1980

School Days

The day broke with an ominous sky, the wind's velocity increased, and the stage was set for a late summer thunderstorm. Wendy appraised her image in the mirror, she was taller than average with breasts larger than average. Her hair was lush, deep dark auburn, Carol thinned her brows, which formed perfect arches over a pair of lively green eyes. Her complexion was creamy ivory, and she would flush easily with emotional changes.

Betty Whitfield was in the kitchen standing over the stove when Wendy entered the room, sensing a presence, her body seemed to jerk until she saw Wendy standing in the doorway, she relaxed, and her face became a beaming reflection of love and joy. The Rev. underestimated his wife, Betty was very well-read. On rare occasions, Wendy and her mother could watch Jeopardy, it amazed Wendy the amount of knowledge her mother possessed. Since the incident on Sunday night, the Rev. had been very scared, if he thought his absence was some sort of punishment, Wendy and her mother were enjoying the void.

The Coates County School was Wendy's destination today as it had been every day for the last eleven years. The trip took her past the dinner, the bank and the clinic on main street before she turned into Apple Avenue which housed the sheriff's office, the firehouse, and the school. The school building was a large two-story, weathered brick building, a large circular drive carved a path in front of the building, and a grassy area filled the inside of the circle with a large plaque that indicated the "Coates County School System". A flight of garnet stairs led to the main entrance; the double doors were standing open as the students arrived for the start of the new school year. Wendy didn't notice any of her friends as she entered the building, the school secretary (Ann) was directing all students to the cafeteria for an assembly, she stopped Wendy and told her she was to report to the principal's office. The principal wanted to issue Wendy her supply closet key, he reminded her only three keys were issued, she noticed Derek Westerkamp was in the office with his father and seemed particularly interested in Wendy's presence.

The cafeteria was full of excited chatter. Wendy spotted Missy and the Anderson twins, and hugs were exchanged as she greeted her old friends. The twins, Cal and Cliff had matured over the summer, they were taller, more muscular, and their faces had taken on a very manly appearance. Missy had changed as well, her braces were gone exposing a beautiful, straight smile, giving her more self-confidence that had been lacking before.

A hush fell over the assembly when Mr. Westerkamp and Derek entered the room, Wendy wasn't sure if the sight and authority of the new principal or the appearance of Derek Westerkamp caused the silence. Low murmuring could be heard throughout the room. Mr. Westerkamp introduced himself, and then the attention turned to Derek's introduction, the murmuring grew in intensity. Derek greeted the crowd, the combination of his Boston drawl, the dazzling smile, the startling blue eyes, and his charm, half of the girls in the school were ready and willing to walk over hot coals for his attention.

The subject of the address to the student body was Mr. Westerkamp's format for the new school year: he started with the Spanish class he would be teaching, the sign-up sheet was posted outside of his office, he explained the hours of school and all students were to exit the building no later than fifteen minutes after the final bell rang, he made sure everyone knew of the exit doors locking after four-thirty, his final point drew a mixed reaction from the crowd, it was the new demerit system. It seemed his demeanour changed slightly when explaining the infractions and punishment of suspension according to the system. Wendy didn't know if it was her imagination or not, but the new principal seemed more intense when speaking of the disciplinary measures that would be applied for physical confrontations.

The assembly was dismissed, Wendy made her way through the crowded hallway to the front of the building and signed-up for the Spanish class Mr. Westerkamp was going to teach. The principal's office was located in the front hall that ran the entire width of the building, the main hall ran through the center of the school with classrooms on both sides and student lockers. The rear corridor housed a flight of steps leading to the second floor, the rear exit, the student's restrooms, the supply/ janitor's closet, and Wendy's locker that she had used since the seventh grade.

Wendy was concentrating on hearing the tumblers of her lock click when she was startled by a tap on her shoulder, she turned and came face to face with a pair of the most beautiful blue eyes she had ever seen. Derek was assigned the locker next to hers, he gave a slow low whistle as he appraised Wendy from head to toe, stopping briefly for an extra-long look at her breasts. Derek's closeness caused a thrill to run through her body, Wendy started to flush, she fumbled for words and couldn't think of a single thing to say. Apparently, Derek was used to the reaction he caused in the opposite sex, as he seemed amused by Wendy's demeanour, the next words he spoke brought her back to a hard reality, "Wow, you sure make life in this jerk town a lot more appealing, by the way what do you do for fun in this one-horse town"? Even though Wendy wanted to leave her hometown, she was offended and angry at his attitude, just a minute ago the eyes she thought were so beautiful, now looked ice cold and cruel. In a voice as cold as Derek's eyes, she told him, "You'll have to ask the horse". Her first encounter with Derek Westerkamp didn't go well, she slammed her locker door closed and left him staring after her as she walked away.

The heavy equipment arrived to break ground for the Blackjack Trucking complex, Jack and Brant were at the site early in the morning. The weather caused a problem when the thunder started to rumble, and lightning streaked the sky; torrential rainfall caused the men to take cover and ride the storm out. Jack decided the break was a good opportunity to pay the Rev. Leroy Whitfield a visit for an informative conversation. Since the evening of the picnic and the verbal abuse the Rev. caused Wendy, Jack knew the time had come for a chat with a man who needed an attitude adjustment. The wipers on Jack's truck were flapping back and forth, labouring to keep the heavy rain from his windshield. Jack turned onto Walnut Avenue, he passed Nan's house, knowing she would be hard at work at the diner, she had started working at the age of seventeen and had been a waitress for the last twenty-eight years, Jack wanted to change that. Jack was tired of the lonely life he had created by the mistakes he had made in his first marriage; he wanted a home and a loving woman to share it with. The Whitfield's house was further up the street, Jack eased his truck along the curb behind the Rev's old station wagon, the rain wasn't falling as hard as before, the doorbell was answered by Betty Whitfield, and she indicated the Rev. was in his church office. If the sudden appearance of Jack requesting the Rev's whereabouts seemed strange to Betty, she hid her reactions well.

Jack pulled the big, heavy doors to the church open and stepped into the vestibule, the last time he had been in the church was when he and Ruby were married. The changes in the church were instantly noticeable to Jack, the rainy weather made the air heavy and damp, the musty aroma seemed to cling to his clothing. The Rev was at his desk with an open Bible lying in front of him, there was no preamble to Jack's greeting with the preacher; he took the seat across the desk, and a sneer curved the Rev's lips as Jack squared his jaw. Jack's voice was low and even, the conversation was one-sided as he spoke for about two minutes, when Jack was finished, the Rev had drained of colour and he was sweating profusely. The Rev's voice was so fierce with anger spittle spewed from his mouth and sprayed his open Bible, "This is blackmail". Jack's voice remained even. "Call it what you want but remember what I said". The chat was over as far as Jack was concerned, he started to the office door, turned and added, "Maybe your next sermon should be about striking the fear of God in sinners". Jack walked down the centre aisle of the church, he started to sing the only hymn he could remember, Onward Christian

Soldier, when he exited, he noticed the sky was clearing, it was time to get back to the construction site.

Sept 15th, Monday 1980

The destructive events occurring at the irrigation ponds on the McKinny farm were causing Brant Miller more than a little concern, the latest was discovered by a farmhand while fishing on Sunday afternoon. Brant, as a young boy had enjoyed the freedom Sam McKinny allowed all the young people of the area, swimming, hiking, and fishing, but now the ponds were going to be posted, No Trespassing, because of the blatant disregard for private property the pond areas would be off limits.

Buzz was in his office when Brant Miller arrived, the two old friends shook hands, Brant sat in the chair across from Buzz and related the latest incident at the pond. A farmhand had found a used condom discarded, while two unused condoms were blown up like balloons tied with a string to a post, empty beer cans and a smashed whisky bottle were strewn about, and evidence of an extinguished fire. The fire was of major concern for Brant, with the approaching fall, the foliage was drying out, an unchecked fire could have devastating consequences. Brant didn't have any alternative but to post the irrigations ponds and would agree to prosecute any trespassers, first the duck with the broken neck now drinking, sex, and an unlawful fire, it was sad to Brant that a few senseless acts could ruin long-standing traditions, and the enjoyment the teens experienced for decades.

After Brant left the sheriff's office, Buzz sent his deputy to post the three irrigation ponds on the McKinny farm, and to check the site of the latest incident for any evidence that may identify a suspect. Identifying a suspect wasn't necessary to Buzz. Hard evidence was another matter, he knew the Westerkamp kid wasn't responsible for the Peeking Tom incidents, those reports were made before the kid's family moved into town, but everything else, Buzz contributed to the kid. There were two things Buzz was counting on, with the postings at the ponds and the threat of prosecution, some of the teens in the area might be angry and come forth with information, the second was the gossip that abounded in a small town. Buzz told Brant about the robbery at Dolly and Mac's small general store, he stopped short of telling Brant that he suspected Derek Westerkamp, but both men agreed, the occurrences on the farm couldn't be taken lightly. Buzz picked up the phone, called the high school office and told Ann he wanted an assembly for Wednesday morning before classes started to address the student body of the destruction of private property. Whether Mr. Westerkamp would agree with Buzz's appearance at the school was of little concern to him, he didn't know the new principal very well, but he didn't like his son.

The weather was beautiful when Wendy left her house for school, not a sign of the approaching fall and harsh winter that followed. She had tried to explain the lipstick her father had found while snooping into her purse, it had nothing to do with vanity. The long walk to school, every day in the cold and unrelenting winds, would cause her lips to chap, lip balms left a coating in her mouth that caused her to gag, the lipstick was a protective measure. Wendy stopped trying to please her father a long time ago, it was an exercise in futility, the Rev referred to the lipstick as the Devil's paint and threw it in the trash, Wendy didn't mean to be disrespectful, just indifferent to her father, she replaced the lipstick. As she approached the school, she hoped that the weekend had calmed the waters between the twins and Derek, Wendy felt guilty, the near confrontation was because of her. Derek was becoming a nuisance; his clumsy, obnoxious attempts at wooing Wendy left her unimpressed and disgusted. He reminded her every girl in school was ready to pull down their panties for him, and it was only a matter of time before she came around to his way of thinking. The prior events of last Friday concerned Wendy, the final bell sounded on Friday, Wendy went to her locker, Derek came up behind her and placed his chin on her shoulder and started to whisper in her ear, she thought she smelled the faint trace of alcohol on his breath which could be the result of mouth wash.

Wendy turned and faced Derek, his face was only inches from her as he pressed close to her, anger and fright coursed through her body. At that instance, Cal and Cliff Anderson appeared in the hall, no words were necessary, the twins lunged at Derek, stopping within inches of bodily contact. The tension was evident, fists were drawn, Derek had a mocking smile on his face while the twins made it clear to leave Wendy alone. Derek tried to goad the twins into a physical confrontation, first with words, hayseeds, farmhands and manure spreaders, then reminding them of who his father was. Cal took the lead and inched closer to Derek, through clenched teeth he told Derek to stay away from Wendy or he would rearrange his pretty boy face. Wendy intervened, the angry situation eased, but she knew the fuses were burnt, the next time would result in an explosion, the hate between the twins and Derek wouldn't have a good ending. Wendy wrote in her journal about the incident and the sexual implications Derek was making toward her, Wendy recognized something about Derek, the only way she could describe his nature in her diary, was dangerous.

Wendy didn't see the twins as she made her way to the rear hallway and her locker, Derek wasn't anywhere to be seen, which was a great relief to her. Her first class of the day was Spanish class. She enjoyed learning the vocabulary, Mr. Westerkamp was also teaching the history of Spain and the South American countries. He would greet his students when passing in the hall, with a simple question in Spanish to see if their response was correct. On Wednesday, he would bring different Spanish dishes for the class to try. Last Wednesday was a taco treat. Wendy wondered how father and son could be so different, the only thing they seemed to have in common was the distinct Boston drawl.

Monday October 20th, 1980

6:45 am.

The day started early for Buzz, and the grain mill was his first stop for an interview with Wayne James Ewing, Sally's father. Henry O'Neil Sr., Buzz's father, owned the mill, and Wayne Ewing was one of his father's best and most trusted employees. Buzz spotted Wayne standing on the dock smoking, talking to a few of his co-workers before their shift was to start at seven o'clock. Buzz only needed a few minutes to interview Wayne, "Wayne, can I have a word with you privately?" the other men discreetly left the dock area. Not knowing if Wayne was aware of his daughter's activities, Buzz broached the subject with caution, "I don't know if you are aware of the assault of Derek Westerkamp on Friday night at the lake on the McKinny's property." "Yes, that's what we were talking about when you arrived." Wayne wasn't acting suspiciously. Buzz was careful, "According to Derek's story, he received a phone call from your daughter on Friday night at eight-thirty, asking him to meet her at the lake for a late-night date." Wayne bristled, "That's impossible, my family left town on Friday after I finished work to visit my sister and her family in Clark County, the county had their Apple Harvest festival, and we were there until yesterday afternoon." Buzz believed Wayne, "I'm sorry I had to ask." Wayne rubbed his jaw as if he was thinking, "Gossip runs rampant in town, but in my opinion, the talk about the Westerkamp kid isn't gossip but gospel, that kid is bad news." Buzz thanked Wayne, he headed to his office, there was a report to file.

The part of the sheriff's job Buzz hated most was the paperwork, his clerical skills were minimal, he picked and plucked on the old typewriter. The phone rang at nine o'clock. Buzz was relived at the interruption until he found out the caller's identity, it was William Westerkamp, "as per your request, I'm calling to inform you the Anderson twins didn't return to school today. This is the second week of their truancy". Buzz was professional and polite with the principal, "Is Derek recovering from his injuries?" "Derek is my business, the Anderson boys' truancy is or should be your business. What are you doing about my son's assault?" Buzz didn't like either of the Westerkamp males, but as Derek's father he had the right to question the progress of the investigation, "All sheriff reports are open to the public, when I finish questioning anyone who might be considered a suspect, and complete my report, I can make you a copy, feel free to pick it up at my office." Buzz heard Westerkamp scoff and the phone connection was broken.

The principal showed little discretion for a professional educator, Buzz turned to the Westerkamp's resume he presented to the school board for employment. Every detail of the resume seemed possible, but Buzz was seriously considering a trip to Boston, it might prove both father and son were liars. Someone posed as Sally to make the phone call, or Derek was lying. Wayne Ewing was eliminated from the list of suspects, now Buzz had to interview Lester Anderson and Cal and Cliff. Lester Anderson was hard core, he was straightforward, to the point, and didn't tolerate anything less from his sons. The Andersons had two daughters but married right out of high school and were in their early twenties, Buzz couldn't imagine either girl getting involved in a teenage drama.

Cal and Cliff had the most reason to harm Derek. Wendy had said Derek was the cause of the fight at school, but the twins weren't given any chance to defend their actions before being suspended.

The Anderson farm was seven miles from Coatesville, and Buzz hoped to catch Lester eating lunch. The house and farm were off the main road. Buzz's Blazer bumped along the long lane, stirring up a cloud of dust. A big Collie dog came to greet Buzz, the aroma of cooking filled the air, the front door was opened by Silva Anderson. Lester and Silva were a few years older than Buzz; the years hadn't been kind to Silva, but her smile reflected the young girl Buzz once knew. "I hate to bother you at mealtime, but I need to speak to Lester and the boys." Silva led Buzz to the kitchen, where Lester had a large hot roast beef sandwich and mashed potatoes on his plate, "Are you hungry Buzz? Silva can fix you a plate of food?" Buzz declined, but the meal sure looked good, and he hadn't eaten since breakfast. Buzz knew Lester liked directness, "Your boys have been absent from school with no excuse, after three days it is considered truancy." Lester looked Buzz straight in the eyes, "My sons are being homeschooled, they will return to classes when the school board realizes the mistake they made in hiring Westerkamp and firing him, only then will Cal and Cliff return to classes." Lester's reaction didn't surprise Buzz, "I noticed your family didn't attend the Harvest Picnic, the folks in town are concerned". "The folks in town like to gossip, and as far as being concerned about my family, maybe they should be concerned about their children and the S.O.B. principle they allow to rule their kids". Lester's anger unruffled Buzz, "Have you heard Derek Westerkamp was the victim of a beating assault on Friday night?" A slight smile formed on Lester's face, "No, I wasn't aware of that, gossip doesn't travel very fast outside of the town limits, so if you are thinking my boys or I had anything to do with the assault, you're wrong, but if you should happen to find out who did beat the kid, extend my gratitude. The boys and I rolled oats over the weekend in addition to our regular farm work, I can assure you we were too tired to beat up a punk kid." Talking to the twins wouldn't serve any purpose, and the Andersons had their story down pat. Buzz talked to Lester and Silva for a while before apologizing for interrupting their meal and the questions he had to ask. Buzz headed to his Blazer and Lester headed to his barn.

The backroom of the sheriff's office had accommodations for occasional overnight duty, the refrigerator was always stocked with sandwich fixings, sodas, and spring water. Buzz was starved upon his arrival at his office; his breakfast seven hours ago was wearing thin, and a three-decker sandwich with a half inch of mayonnaise was just the ticket to tide him over until supper.

Buzz cleared the desktop and began to lay out every note he had gathered, starting with the IGA robbery, the thirty pictures Gus took at the Harvest Picnic were examined closely. Someone was twenty-two hundred dollars richer and money talks. Any picture with a stranger attending the picnic was placed on a separate pile, Buzz planned a trip to Honee's House. Perhaps the strangers could be identified by the girls working at the "Gentlemen Club".

Buzz turned his attention to the assault of Derek, he made notes on all his interviews: Brant Miller, Dr. Bender, Derek Westerkamp, Wayne Ewing, and Lester Anderson. The notes were compared, Buzz wasn't ready to eliminate Cal and Cliff

Anderson as possible suspects. Judge Krebs wouldn't issue a search warrant without probable cause, no such evidence existed. Lester Anderson could agree to a property search without a warrant, but what would Buzz find? Perhaps an old plastic wiffleball bat or a sock and sand somewhere on the farm, both items could have been used as weapons. If Derek had been unconscious during the beating, the assailants wouldn't have any defensive injuries. The Anderson farm was seven miles from Coatesville, if Cal and Cliff committed the crime, they probably wouldn't have walked to the lake. Judge Krebs and Buzz had locked horns on several occasions, the Judge believed in due process of the law, Buzz believed some instances call for retribution, and the twins certainly had cause.

4:00.

Wendy had a very bad day at school, gossip was whispered throughout the school all day, the principal was in a foul mood, and Derek and the twins were absent from classes.

Buzz caught Wendy as she passed the sheriff's office, walking home, "Wendy, do you have a few minutes to spare?" "Sure, I'm not working at Carol's salon today." Wendy had no doubt what Buzz wanted to talk to her about this time. Wendy didn't need any prompting from Buzz. She was ready to talk, "I feel terrible, I blame myself for the twins' truancy and their suspension. If Cal and Cliff beat Derek because of the suspension, I feel responsible for the assault. Most of the girls feel I'm responsible and won't speak to me anymore, the principal sneered at me all day, and my Spanish class was a nightmare. On top of that, I saw my father sneaking through the graveyard last night, dressed in dark clothing!" Buzz's attention was on full alert, "Are you sure it was your father and what do you mean by sneaking?" Wendy was almost in tears, "I couldn't sleep last night, I heard about Derek's beating from Brant Miller at the Dog-Do yesterday. I didn't want to believe the twins were guilty, but I'm to blame if they were. It was after eleven o'clock, I got up to close my bedroom window, I saw a man, I recognized my father by his gait, he was sneaking through the graveyard, heading to the back entrance of the church. He was walking rapidly when he entered the church, I knew for sure it was my father. I lay awake until one o'clock, wondering if my father was the "Peeping Tom." Buzz wanted to say something to reassure Wendy, but he was thinking the same thing, with everything that had been happening in the county, he had forgotten the "Peeping Tom" incidents. There hadn't been any more reports filed lately, either the Rev. was getting very good at being undetected or there was another explanation for the Pastor's strange behavior. "Please don't blame yourself, I really believe there was an instant hatred between Derek and the twins, the hatred was bound to erupt at some point in time. Even if you weren't present to witness the fight, the twins would have been suspended anyway. I talked to Lester Anderson today, Cal and Cliff are being homeschooled and will not return to classes while William Westerkamp is the principal. Lester said the boys were home all weekend and they didn't know about the assault. Can you tell me of any other girls Derek is dating besides Sally Ewing?" Wendy thought for a moment, "I don't really know, most of the girls Derek is interested in are underclassmen, there is a little talk about Leslie Patterson. Leslie and Sally used to be best friends but now they hate each other." "Wendy, please keep everything we discussed today between you and me, including your suspicions about your father." Wendy agreed.

Buzz was ready to call it a day, the trip he planned to Honee's House might prove to be very interesting.

Tuesday October 21st, 1980

6:00 am.

Tuesday didn't start as Buzz planned; the alarm went off at six o'clock, but his body didn't respond. Chills engulfed his body, his head felt like it was about to explode, and his energy drained. The cooking aroma coming from the kitchen was making him nauseous, he laid back on the bed and the whole room seemed to be spinning. He heard movement in the hallway, he called out, which caused his head to pound, his eyes even hurt. During his military time, he had been hungover a few times. Today, his symptoms were similar, and he felt like the morning after too much cheap whiskey. Betsy hollered from the kitchen, "Breakfast is ready," when Buzz didn't respond, she appeared in the doorway. Her husband was as pale as a ghost and sick as a dog.

Betsy went into nursing mode, she got a thermometer, three Tylenol, and a cool wet rag for Buzz's forehead, she made him as comfortable as possible, his temperature was a hundred-two degrees. It was too early for Dr. Bender to be in the clinic. Betsy left a message on his answering machine asking him to call her back, the Tylenol must have worked, and Buzz was sound asleep.

Dr. Bender called about eight o'clock, "My waiting room is sitting full, the flu is running rampant. There isn't any cure, treat the symptoms, pain reliever, a liquid diet, and plenty of rest. Most cases last about four days. When Buzz's appetite returns the worst is probably over, if the symptoms last longer than a week, have him come to the clinic. Don't let your children have any contact with their father." Betsy checked on her husband, he was still asleep, and she needed a hot cup of coffee.

4:00 pm.

Wendy's mood went from bad to worse as the school day progressed, all of Derek's groupies were thrilled when they found out he was returning to school on Thursday. Derek was the reason Cal and Cliff weren't in school, she didn't care if he ever returned. So many things were changing in Wendy's life, senior year was supposed to be the best and most exciting year of school, now she dreaded every day. Calvin asked Wendy to their senior prom, which probably wouldn't happen, and her senior trip didn't excite her as it once had. Middle Tennessee State University offered her a scholarship, but Wendy was starting to rethink her decision to attend a college so far from home.

Wendy headed to Carol's salon, she had a lot to enter in her journal, and she wanted to talk to Carol. Carol seemed like a second mother to Wendy, she listened and only offered advice when asked. Secrets were safe with Carol, but some things Wendy kept to herself and her diary.

The salon wasn't busy on Tuesdays, and Carol was overjoyed when Wendy got there, "Mike called, he's coming home to stay". Wendy felt a pang of quilt, she was relieved Mike finally told Carol of his decision to leave the military, she hated keeping secrets from Carol. The expression on Carol's face changed, Wendy felt so selfish, "Do you want to talk about whatever is bothering you?" "I'm thinking about turning down the scholarship to MTSU and opting for a school much closer to home, part of the reason is my mother, I'm the only source of love she has, and my priorities are changing as well. I would like to have a home and family, I see happy couples all around me. What's wrong with being a postal worker, a bank teller or learning a trade like you?" Carol dreaded the day Wendy would leave Coatesville for college, so she had to be careful and not let her selfishness taint her reply, "Priorities change, mine changed out of necessity. I wanted to be a journalist all my life, I worked for Gus at the newspaper office while I was in high school. I hoped to be a foreign correspondent or go to New York City and work for a big publishing paper like the Post. I had to drop out of college in my sophomore year because my mother contracted Multiple Sclerosis, after she died, I had Mike to raise. I never regretted my decision, my business is successful. I just married the man I fell in love with, and we are hoping to adopt a child. The decisions you make will affect the rest of your life, I'm almost sure your mother wouldn't want to hold you back, but if you are hesitating, I would think you have already made up your mind. Careers in banking or postal service have a lot of room for advancement. There are several accredited colleges within traveling distance, if you were given a scholarship from a college like MTSU, any college would accept you. Tell me, are you thinking of anyone special to have a home and family with?" Wendy wasn't sure about that either, "In the past year, my feelings for Calvin Anderson have changed from a good friend to wanting to date him." Carol smiled, "Their father has always been a very handsome man, he's older than I am but I see him and his boys in town, the twins resemble Lester."

9:00 pm.

Wendy finished her homework, she sat by the window looking out at the dark, sad cemetery, if her father was the "Peeping Tom" the dark clothing he was wearing would be hidden in the church, she was going to do a little more snooping.

Monday October 27ᵗʰ, 1980

7:00 am.

It wasn't until Monday that Buzz was finally back in the Sheriff's office, as strong as he was the flu left him flat on his back for four days. The first meal he shared with his family was Saturday night supper, he had lost six pounds while being sick, but his appetite returned with a vengeance. There were six messages on the answering machine when he got to the office, all the calls were from William Westerkamp. With each unanswered message, the principal's tone became more agitated, accusing Buzz of purposely avoiding him; Buzz took his time getting in touch with Westerkamp. Buzz didn't offer an explanation as to why he wasn't in his office the prior week, the only possible explanation Westerkamp would have accepted as valid was if Buzz was dead.

10:00 am.

It was ten o'clock when Buzz turned onto the long tree-lined driveway leading to a very large, two-story Victorian-style house that dated to the eighteenth century. A wrap-around porch was sitting full of white wicker furniture, the large oak door was opened by the madam of the "Gentleman's Club". Honee was a lovely woman in her late forties or early fifties, dressed in what looked like a very expensive pants suit, her voice was a slow southern drawl, "Why sheriff honey, I didn't know you would partake in such pleasures, but darlin we don't open until four o'clock." The gentlemen's club was the worst kept secret in the county, the southern drawl was as fake as a seven-dollar bill, Buzz happened to know Honee came from the northeast to escape an abusive pimp. The pimp got Honee hooked on hard drugs, she walked the streets and turned tricks to feed her habit, all the while making big money for her pimp. Honee made her way to this area, she had long since given up turning tricks but had rescued girls caught in the same scenario, brought them here and off the streets. The girls were very grateful and loyal to Honee, some of them owed her their lives, hooking on the streets could be dangerous, they kicked their habits, and were provided with housing and a safer working environment. Each girl was required to get an education, a hooking career lasted about ten years before men preferred younger, more agile women. The girls had a strict routine, two and a half hours of physical exercise daily, schooling, and a medical exam each month, testing for STD and any other problems resulting from the business Honee operated.

Buzz was out of his element, "I would like to speak to your girls in reference to the possible identification of a suspect." Honee checked her wristwatch, "The girls are in physical training right now, you know, training that keeps their bodies lean and easy to look at, they will be done in fifteen minutes, you can wait in the parlor if you want." Buzz blushed, he was led into a very large room, a massive bar covered the one wall, stocked with every kind of whiskey available, displayed on mirrored shelves. The parlor had groupings of furniture that would enable the ladies to entertain clients with a drink and casual conversation before heading to the second floor. The rules for the clientele were unspoken but understood: no drinking above the first-floor area, no S&M, no sex toys, or abuse, any client violating the rules would be escorted off the property with a NO Return policy.

Buzz wasn't comfortable in his surroundings but sat on a sofa and wondered how many men prior to him had sat here waiting for the ladies to come down the stairs. Hearing low voices and laughter made Buzz look up the stairs to see four beautiful young women who looked nothing like the image one gets of a hooker. Each girl had a distinctive look that was different from the others, without the heavy make-up and the flimsy clothing, Buzz thought they looked as respectable as any of the women in Coatesville. The girls were well-spoken, not loud and brassy like the girl Clark Taylor had living with him, the girls didn't use their real names, "Spring" had the appearance of an All-American girl next door look, "Summer" looked like a Malibu Barbie, "Autumn" had deep auburn hair and pale green eyes, and "Winter" had dark hair, dark skin, and dark eyes. Buzz told the girls the reason for his visit and pulled out the photos of the Harvest Picnic with a circle drawn around the men he wanted identified, "Have you ever seen any of the men circled in the pictures?" Winter seemed to be the spokesperson, "You do understand that most of our clients use an alias when visiting, and most men aren't forthcoming with personal or professional information, but we will help any way we can." Each girl examined the pictures. Spring recognized one man who identified himself as a "Snook" when visiting and was a construction worker from Center County. Buzz asked them to look at the picture of the Westerkamp family, "Have you ever seen this boy?" Autumn stunned Buzz, "I don't recognize the boy but the man in the picture is a regular client, he visits at least once a week, he goes by the name "Nelson", he's a strange duck." "What do you mean by strange?" Autumn was candid, "Nelson prefers red hair so he always chooses me, he has two drinks and just stares at me, no conversation, when we go up-stairs, he lays on the bed and watches me brush my hair for fifteen minutes, when he gets sexually aroused he reeks of "Garlic", the odor is overpowering and make me nauseous, I have to spray my room and open all the windows when he leaves. I can't stand the smell of garlic anymore. The rate is fifty dollars for an hour visit, but he always gives me a ten-dollar tip." Buzz didn't want to alarm Autumn "If Nelson returns for another visit, act as though we never had this conversation." Autumn's voice was concerned, "Is Nelson dangerous?" Buzz knew Westerkamp wouldn't do anything to expose his identity, "No, but if he does anything out of the ordinary in his visits, please contact me." Buzz thanked the girls and left; he pondered the info from every angle as he traveled back to his office.

There wasn't anything against the law using an alias at a brothel, especially for a married man or principal of a school district, but Buzz had suspicions about the Westerkamp men for a long time. Something wasn't right. Every alarm was screaming in Buzz's mind, it was time for some answers. Before he arrived back at his office the decision was made to go to Boston. There were a few loose ends that Buzz had to consider, but he planned to book a flight out of the small airport in Wayne County to Chicago then to Boston.

4:00 pm.

When Derek returned to school after the assault, he completely ignored Wendy, there wasn't any snide remarks about the twins or any suggestive behavior toward her. On the few occasions they came face to face while visiting their lockers, Derek acted as though Wendy didn't exist. Mr. Westerkamp was over his snit, his attitude changed, and once again, Spanish class was a pleasant learning experience.

Monday was unseasonably warm; the student body was eager to get outdoors when the final bell sounded. It was the end of the month, Wendy wanted to do a full inventory of the supply closet, a requisition form would be filled out and given to the secretary. The supply closet was also the storage area for the janitorial supplies, two large sinks were in the corner, the smell of the closet had become so familiar to Wendy over the years. Banana oil was used on the dust mops the janitors used on the old wooden floors of the school. The closet's walls were twelve feet high, the only light the room had come from two rows of fluorescent light fixtures attached to the ceiling. The days were much shorter this time of year and the closet was extremely hot, Wendy wanted to get her work done as soon as possible.

Tim and Ed worked for the school district all their lives, they were always very pleasant and cheerful with Wendy, they returned their dust mops to the closet and bid Wendy a good day. Mr. Westerkamp was probably still in his office, without Derek to pester her, Wendy was relaxed as she went about her work.

Suddenly the room went pitch black, Wendy sensed a rush of motion behind her, Wendy's eyes didn't have a chance to adjust to the darkness, when she heard a familiar Boston drawl hissing in her ear, "The beating was your fault." A crushing blow from an elbow came down on the small of her neck, and everything went dark for Wendy.

Wendy started to regain consciousness, but panic struck her. She wondered if she was still in danger, so she remained on the floor, keeping very still and listening as she tried to get her eyes to focus on the darkness. Realizing she was alone, Wendy tried to sit up, her mind was racing, her body wasn't responding to her commands, finding the strength she found the light switch, the instant brightness hurt her eyes. The room came into focus, Wendy was appalled, all her undergarments were strewn on the floor, she knew then she had suffered more than a blow to her neck, she had been raped. A wave of nausea came over Wendy, she stumbled to the sink and vomited, racking sobs that sounded like a wounded animal soon replaced the retching. Hatred racked Wendy's body when she pulled up her skirt and saw a clear slime mixed with strands of blood running down the inside of her legs. The damage was extensive, she could see bruising starting to form on her inter thighs and the pain was agonizing. Wendy grabbed some rags from the janitor's closet, with some warm water, started to clean herself, rage gripped her soul, and she thought no amount of washing would ever make her feel clean again. Up until now, Wendy was a virgin, she often fantasized about what it would be like to make love for the first time with a man she loved. The rape that happened to her had nothing to do with love, just hate, and now she hated Derek Westerkamp, he had warned her, but she didn't think he would ever be capable of such cruelty.

Wendy became aware of the time, knowing she had to get home before someone came looking for her, now she had a much bigger problem on her hands, there wasn't a single soul she could tell. She hurried and replaced everything in the closet, put the soiled rags and underwear in her bookbag and practically ran out of the school and headed home.

By the time Wendy arrived home, she was in agonizing pain, she didn't lie to her mother, she had vomited at school, had broken into a cold sweat, and felt nauseous, the symptoms painted a false picture of the flu. Wendy was able to escape to her upstairs haven, she bathed in very hot water, scrubbing herself over and over, wondering if she would ever feel clean again. When the water started to cool, she slipped into some PJs and got into bed.

The pain Wendy was experiencing from the brutal rape was second to the anger and hate she felt, and the shame was overwhelming, the words Derek said echoed in her mind, "The beating was your fault." she assessed the bruising on her upper thigh, clothing would hide her shame, but the mental anguish would never go away, hot tears turned to deep sobs, Wendy worried about her sanity. Wendy's thoughts turned to panic, what if as a result of the rape, she would be pregnant? Fear caused another bout of nausea.

Wendy didn't have a single option available, there wasn't one person she could talk to about the terrible trauma she had suffered at the hands of Derek Westerkamp, her greatest fear was her father would find out and label her a "whore". Wendy laid awake in her dark bedroom, her whole life changed on October 27th, she decided to enter the whole rape incident in her journal, which was as close as she could get to sharing the rape.

November 1980 Coatesville

It was business as usual in Coatesville, "Blackjack Trucking Company was a reality, Jack Furry was a decent hardworking man who recognized two things, addictions and talent. Todd Baker had both, he had a drinking problem and was an ace mechanic, Jack offered Todd a job in his new company. Jack had lost his wife and children because of his gambling habit; he didn't want that to happen to Todd because of his drinking. Jack had two rules he placed on Todd's employment, never to drink on the job, or come to work hungover, it was a win for both men, Jack got an ace mechanic and short-haul trucker while Todd was drying out with regular pay for his family.

Nan and Jack were living together in Nan's house, she was still at the diner but planned to leave her employment when Jack's new house was completed at the company's site. Jack loved having a woman to share his home and live with, Nan was going to help with the company's paperwork while pursuing her passions, cooking and gardening.

Bill Miller, Brant's father, suffered a mild myocardial infarction and was recovering under the watchful eyes of Ty and Sueme. The adoption papers for Sueme were finalized and she was now a member of the Miller family. Ty's pregnancy was obvious, and was going well, the old demons she had of all the tragedies surrounding her family were gone.

Tom joined Jack's trucking company, he enjoyed the short-run hauls and being at home with his new wife. Carol's salon was as busy as ever, she was excited Mike would be home to stay around Thanksgiving. Tom and Carol had their first interview at an adoption agency, their background and financial records met the standards, and they were placed on a list as candidates.

Evonne's love life was heating up, and it was ironic that the man she was falling in love with was responsible for ending her marriage to Clark Taylor. Robert Newman was a brilliant lawyer who maintained a very low profile, one of the qualities Evonne found attractive. The couple were planning a Thanksgiving Holiday visit to Evonne's parents' home in the deep northwest.

Buzz had to postpone his trip to Boston for a week, his three children came down with the flu, Betsy had her hands full, and he wasn't going to ask his wife to shoulder all the responsibility in his absence.

Friday November 1st, 1980

Wendy took three days off from school under the pretense of having the flu, it was a blessing she didn't have a fever, her mother would have insisted on a trip to the clinic. When Wendy started her walk to school, the weather was a mixture of rain and sleet. Everywhere she looked life was going on as usual, time was standing still for her, she was lost in the moment of the rape. The diner was sitting full, people smiling, and talking as they enjoyed their breakfast. Each step took Wendy closer to her destination, Wendy's legs felt like rubber when she turned the corner at Apple Ave, the school loomed in the distance, she seemed to be on the verge of collapsing. The bruises caused by the rape were starting to fade, the physical pain had subsided, but her mental state hadn't improved, no amount of time could ease what happened to her in the building she was nearing.

By the time Wendy climbed the granite steps to the entrance, she was hyperventilating, and her anger swelled her chest. Anne, the school secretary, was at her desk, Wendy didn't want to engage in a lengthy conversation, "Here's my written excuse from my mother for the three days of absents, I won't be taking care of the supply closet any longer, I am dropping my Spanish class, I want to replace it with a study hall, and I want another locker assigned to me." Wendy laid the written excuse on Ann's desk along with the key to the supply closet she had been issued and walked out of the office. Ann stared after Wendy in disbelief, the sweet girl she had known for many years seemed to be gone.

The happy chatter coming from the students visiting their lockers seemed distant as Wendy walked down the hall like a zombie, there were people all around her, but she couldn't focus on the faces. When she turned the corner to the rear hall, sheer panic and terror gripped her soul, there before Wendy at the end of the hall was the supply closet. The sight of the closet caused the nightmare of her rape to come flooding back in her mind, Wendy stopped in her tracks, bile raised in her throat, she clenched her fist into tight balls, with an overpowering desire to scream and flee the building. Wendy's locker was halfway down the hall, she willed herself to move, every sense was on full alert, her nerve ends were pricking her skin, dying right there would have been a blessing.

Derek moved up beside her at his locker, the hatred Wendy felt radiated from her body, she wanted to beat him until her anger subsided, she wished whoever assaulted him before would have beaten him to DEATH. Hot tears stung Wendy's eyes as she made her way to her first class.

The day dragged on, Wendy no longer dreaded school, she hated it, skipping lunch she opted for a walk around the building. Between each class Wendy went into the restroom hoping to find signs of her menstrual period was about to start, but there wasn't any evidence found, with each bathroom visit Wendy became more desperate.

Wendy's concentration was gone, once while in English class, she heard her name being called in a sharp tone, she jerked back to reality to see her teacher looking at her sternly and her classmates staring in her direction. "Miss Whitfield, are you with us today, I know you were out of school due to illness, if you are still not feeling well, you can be excused from class." Wendy managed a slight nod of her head, "no, I'm fine, what was the question?"

The final bell sounded, Missy Evans caught up to Wendy at her locker, "You are my best friend, I can tell something is wrong with you, I didn't even see you at lunch." Wendy's voice was quaking, and her words were short and breathless. "Nothing wrong, I've just got to get out of here." she brushed past Missy and practically ran out of the rear exit of the school.

4:15 pm.

The biggest test would be facing Carol for the first time since the rape, Wendy was relieved to see the salon was busy when she arrived. Mrs. Lewis was in the chair, Carol was doing her comb-out, "Hey Wendy, I sure missed you." Wendy didn't have any reason to doubt Carol's feelings for her. With the best smile she could muster, Wendy made her response seem light and cheerful, "I'm feeling much better and ready to go back to work." Wendy made her escape from the room as quickly as possible, she put a load of soiled towels in the washer, new supplies had arrived in her absence, so she replenished the storage cupboards, but she really wanted to make an entry in her journal. Carol had one more client to finish, Wendy knew she would be undisturbed as she recorded her nightmare in the notebook.

On Monday, October 27th, I was raped by Derek Westerkamp in the supply closet at school. The lights went out, I couldn't see anything, Derek came up behind me, with his strong Boston Drawl, and hissed in my ear, "You caused the beating." he was blaming me for his assault. He knocked me over the head, I must have passed out, when I regained consciousness, I realized I had been raped, and I sensed something else, the strong smell of Garlic. I thought it was my imagination, but the odor lingered in the closed closet, overpowering the usual smell of banana oil. I can't stand the smell of garlic anymore, I am frantic awaiting my period, I pray I'm not pregnant. My deepest fear is my father finding out about the rape, he must never know, he will blame me for being a wanton woman that he talks about in his sermons. I would become a disgrace to him, a damaged daughter and labeled a whore. I cannot confide in a single person; every avenue would lead straight to my father. I feel so alone and ashamed. A few tears dropped on her journal pages as Wendy finished the last sentence.

Sunday November 3rd, 1980

Sharp cold winds whipped through the old cemetery, scattering the fallen leaves, Wendy watched from her bedroom window, sleep would have provided her with some relief from her torment, but her mind was in a constant battle with what her body longed for. Time was becoming Wendy's enemy, if she was pregnant, in a few months from now, it would become evident, and her shame would be complete.

Wendy had decisions to make, her options were minimal, she thought about going to the clinic, Dr. Bender would be bound to the doctor-patient confidentiality oath. If the pregnancy test proved positive, Wendy would have to explain her sexual activity was nonconsensual, and since she was a minor, would Dr. Bender be bound to report the crime of rape. Abortion sounded foreign to Wendy, she envisioned a conception of love, this child would have been conceived in hate and revenge. The extra money Wendy had stashed at Carol's salon was five hundred plus dollars, she considered running away, but where suicide crossed her mind, it would put an end to her agony.

The sky was starting to brighten on the eastern horizon, dawn was breaking, and it was another sleepless night for Wendy. She hadn't solved a single problem she was facing.

8:30 am.

Wendy had her weekly pre-service chores to perform, nothing seemed important anymore, she didn't snoop in her father's notebook or search for the dark clothing she suspected was hidden in the church. Wendy did something she hadn't done in a very long time, she knelt at the altar and begged God to either let her die or send her some guidance, she wept uncontrollably.

9:00.

The congregation was sparse, the cold wind rattled the old church windows, Wendy splashed cold water on her face and resumed the seat in her regular pew, ready to play the part of the preacher's daughter.

1:00 pm.

Buzz's entire family was at the table for Sunday dinner, and the children had all recovered from the same flu that had left him flat on his back for four days. The trip to Boston was now Buzz's top priority, the travel plans were all confirmed, he would be leaving tomorrow. Buzz was starting to question his Sheriff's position, he looked at his children gathered at the table and realized how much of their lives he had missed and all the responsibility he had placed on his wife in their thirteen-year marriage. Henry O'Neil Sr. wanted to retire, he owned and operated the feed and grain mill; the business would be Buzz's someday, and he wondered if now wasn't the time to change careers.

Monday November 4th, 1980

Wendy was walking toward the Hell she found herself living in since the rape, she was totally unaware of people she passed or the harsh wind howling all around. The school looked cold and cruel as she approached. The familiar sound of the old heating pipes clanging and bringing heat from the basement greeted Wendy as she entered the building.

Ann called out to Wendy as she passed the office, "Wendy, I need to see you for a few minutes. I have your new locker assignment, it is on the second floor with the freshmen and sophomores, your request for a study hall to replace Spanish class will be on the second floor as well. Mr. Westerkamp was very concerned with the abrupt changes you requested; he may want to speak to you later."

Wendy had to visit her old locker one last time to retrieve the contents, suddenly Derek was standing beside her, "Wendy, I want to say I'm sorry." Before Derek could form another sentence, Wendy turned on him, her eyes were glazed over with hate, her teeth were clenched and her fists formed tight balls, in a fierce voice that could cut diamonds, "YOUR SORRY, YOUR SORRY, if you ever touch me again, I'll kill you", Wendy snapped, she had to escape, exiting the rear entrance, she begun to run. Wendy realized she was running blindly, but where, she thought her last shred of sanity was gone, returning to school was the only thing she could do. The rear exit was unlocked during regular school hours, she entered the building the same way she had exited, thinking no one would be any wiser, Derek wasn't anywhere in sight, she gathered her belongings and went upstairs to locate her new locker.

12:00 Noon.

Buzz parked his Blazer in the small airport's garage, grabbed his suitcase and checked in at the ticket counter, his scheduled flight to O'Hare International was leaving at one-fifteen. The commuter plane was small and cramped, and Buzz felt like his knees were practically in his face. The flight was short, which was a blessing, it seemed as though the plane no sooner reached its recommended attitude until the announcement was made to prepare for landing.

O'Hare International Airport had grown since Buzz's military time, it was a maze of mass chaos, he recognized three different languages being used, lines formed at every counter, with conveyor belts moving luggage in every direction, and arrivals and departures being announced every five minutes.

Buzz departed at four o'clock, the flight was one hour and forty-eight minutes, the seat he occupied had more legroom, he used his airtime to review the picture and resume of William Westerkamp.

Logan International was a much smaller version of O'Hare, but Buzz was still lost in a world of busy travelers. Buzz's travel allocation funds from the Sheriff's budget were limited, he opted for the cheapest accommodations he could book, the old saying, "You get what you pay for," rang true when he saw his motel room. The ice maker was in the hall, the room was small with a double bed with a cheap flowered quilt, a small television was on top of a three-drawer dresser. The shower was a small cabinet like cubicle that hardly accommodated Buzz's large frame, the motel didn't offer room service, but there were plenty of laminated menus from various area restaurants lying on top of the dresser. The delivery charges were outrageous and outweighed the price of a meal, but Buzz didn't have much choice but to order in, his whole Sheriff's pay wouldn't be enough for an extended stay in Boston. Buzz ordered a BLT with FF and coffee, he unpacked his few clothes and headed for a cramped shower. The meal arrived promptly; it was hot and tasty, but the total bill with delivery and tip was thirty-one dollars. Buzz decided he needed to diet while in Boston.

Buzz was homesick already, he placed a call to Betsy at eight o'clock, which would be seven o'clock in Coatesville, he could hear his children in the background expressing their love and how much they missed him. Betsy was apprehensive, she had heard a large storm was heading east, he reassured her, his return flight was departing from Logan at five fifteen the following day.

Buzz needed a good night of sleep, the television's reception was lousy, with only a few channels to choose from, the walls of his room were an ugly green and the door was painted a bright orange, he closed his eyes and hoped not to have nightmares, he missed home and his loving wife more than ever.

Tuesday November 5th, 1980

Boston 10:00 am.

There was a coffee vending machine in the motel lobby, Buzz grabbed a cup and paid a dollar for the worst "Joe" he had ever tasted. The movies provided Buzz with an example of how to hail a taxi in a big city, it seemed cabs outnumbered personal vehicles three to one on the busy street. Once Buzz settled in the taxi he handed the address of his destination to the cabbie, the driver accelerated with such force it threw Buzz back in his seat. The cabbie told Buzz his destination was over ten miles across the city, and that he might want to opt for a cheaper mode of transportation for the return to his motel.

The driver was right, the one-way fare to the prep school was twenty-two dollars not including the tip.

After traveling about six miles through streets lined with massive buildings and bustling ado, the landscape started to change, very vast estates with luxury cars parked in circular driveways and open-air parks started to dot the landscape. The cabbie explained that this section of Boston was home to industrial moguls; signs appeared everywhere for the Boston Red Sox, Boston Celtics, and Boston College Eagles. The whole area screamed affluent people reside here. When the cab came to a halt, Buzz saw a very prestigious Prep School that reeked of money. Climbing the long flight of marble stairs to the oversized front door, Buzz couldn't help thinking, this building alone was larger than the whole senior high school in Coatesville. The lobby was vast, with marble floors, highly polished wood paneling, and huge brass lamp fixtures, a woman appeared out of nowhere, she appraised Buzz, looking him up and down as if he were an alien, "May I help you?" Buzz requested, "I would like to talk to the school principal." The woman had a complete look of disgust on her face, she sneered at Buzz as if he was joking, "This is an academy, we don't have a principal, just a dean of girls or a dean of boys." At that point Buzz had enough of the up-tight bitches' attitude, he pulled out his badge and the most condescending voice he could muster, "I don't care which Dean I speak to, this is not a student-related matter." The woman bristled, "Neither dean will be available until two o'clock, you can wait or return then if you wish."

Buzz was hungry, but he knew better than to try to get something to eat in this part of town, he wandered the street for an hour and returned to the school at two o'clock. The same woman was annoyed by Buzz's return, her distain was apparent, she ushered him into an office where he was told in a most impatient voice, "Wait here; the dean will be with you shortly." The office was just as impressive as the lobby, with fine art and busts of different important people, he noticed a painting of Paul Revere and his famous horse, "Brown Beauty" rearing up while Paul held one lantern. When the office door finally opened, forty-five minutes had passed, and while Buzz was expecting a man, a woman introduced herself as Miss Franklin, dean of girls. Miss Franklin was just what Buzz pictured as the dean of an elite prep school, her hair was pulled straight back, tied in a tight knot, she was dressed in what looked like a uniform complete with a crest on her jacket and a tie. Miss Franklin proved to be as snotty as the office woman, and didn't hesitate to show her scorn, "I understand you are a sheriff, this academy has never had a whiff of sandal or any illegal issues, so I wish you would state your business and be on your way." "I am not here to bring shame to your academy", Buzz replied, "I'm here to check on the information in the resume Mr. William Westerkamp submitted to our school board when applying for the position as principal in our county."

The next statement by Miss Franklin stunned Buzz, "I'm sure you must have a mistaken identity, Mr. William Westerkamp that taught here has been dead for almost two years. He also refereed the girls' basketball games, during one of those games, he had a heart attack and was dead before he hit the floor." By the time Miss Franklin finished, Buzz was staring at her in disbelief, he pulled out the picture he had gotten from Gus and placed it in front of the woman sitting across from him, "Do you know the identity of the man in this picture?" Miss Franklin stared at the picture for only a few moments, "Yes, that is William Nelson, he did work her but in the capacity of a janitor; our board of directors dismissed him. Some of our female students had concerns about his behavior. As far as I know, his whole family left Boston under a cloud of suspicion, something about his son Steven and an underaged girl." Buzz's mind was on red alert, "how old would Steven have been at the time?" Miss Franklin thought, "He was a senior in another school in the area at the time of the family's departure; that was two years ago, so I guess he would be about twenty or twenty-one by now." Everything became clear to Buzz, "Did William Westerkamp have a son"? Buzz was almost sure he knew the answer, "Yes, Derek, he was a bright boy, he took his dad's death hard, at the time, he was only sixteen, he is now a senior at a boy's prep school here in Boston." The picture was clear, if the real Westerkamp had a son, to fit the profile of the resume, Steven Nelson had to pose as Derek Westerkamp, entering his senior year. Buzz asked Miss Franklin if he could obtain copies of both Nelson and Westerkamp personnel file, he knew she probably would discover one of the files was gone. True to form, when Miss Franklin returned to her office, she seemed puzzled, "The file on William Westerkamp has disappeared." It wasn't a bit surprising to Buzz, the fake Westerkamp had removed the file before his departure, he needed a new identity.

The time Buzz spent at the prep school was longer than anticipated, once again he opted for a cab, his return flight from Logan was scheduled to leave at five-fifteen. Buzz climbed the old motel staircase two steps at a time, he stuffed his belongings in the suitcase, he never wanted to see the ugly wallpaper of his rented room again. The motel clerk seemed bored and nodded farewell when Buzz checked out, eating was costly, but his stomach was about to rebel, he got a sandwich and coffee to go at the closest café, hailed a cab, he was on his way home.

4:00 Coatesville.

Wendy waited in the restroom until most of the students left the school, she didn't want to share the shame of being summoned to the principal's office. She received a note while in English class from Mr. Westerkamp, requesting her to report to his office after school. Wendy thought the English teacher had informed the principal of her inattentive behavior the prior day.

Wendy had made some decisions, she was no longer fearful, she planned to tell Buzz about her rape, she had tried all her life to seek her father's love and approval, it had never worked. The brutal rape wasn't her fault, she understood that fact now, the rape was a vicious crime and Derek was going to pay. The Rev. could disown her or whatever he found necessary, but she couldn't shoulder the shame and trauma on her own any longer. The fear Wendy once felt had turned to unabated anger, while on her way to the office, she stopped and stared at the supply closet, for the first time she was able to face her past.

Ann was gone from her office, and a note on the principal's door read, "I will be back as soon as possible, please wait." Wendy surveyed the office, a picture of the smiling faces of the Westerkamp family was displayed on the desk, Wendy's nostrils flared with anger, she wanted to smash the glass and destroy the photo.

A half-hour lapsed, and Wendy didn't care if she was late getting home, she didn't care if the principal was concerned about her failing grades or lack of attention in class. Wendy wanted Derek to make the mistake of touching her again, so she could claw his snug face and end his ugly Boston drawl, she wanted to embarrass her father by being an unmarried pregnant whore, she dared anyone to stand in her way. The office was growing dim, Wendy was ready to leave assuming the principal had forgotten the meeting, then she heard footsteps in the hall. Mr. Westerkamp appeared in the office doorway, he apologized for being late, "Sorry to keep you waiting, there was a problem with the old boiler, I hope the school district approves the money for a new heating system." Wendy noticed his white shirt sleeves were rolled up to the elbow, his hands were dirty, and his red stripped tie was undone hanging around his neck, Wendy didn't acknowledge his apology or return his greeting, she sat staring at the horrid picture on his desk and listened. There was a private bathroom in the office, Mr. Westerkamp kept up a steady stream of conversation in that Boston drawl that made her skin crawl while he cleaned up. Wendy sat silently, waiting for the reason for the meeting, she had answers ready for any inquiries the principal might have, "It's none of your business," was going to be her response. The first question stunned Wendy, "by the way did you tell anyone about the rape?" Wendy became paralyzed with fear, she looked at his sick twisted smile, and suddenly smelled the overpowering odor of garlic, she knew it wasn't Derek who had raped her, it was William Westerkamp. Wendy's adrenaline was pumping, she had to escape somehow, jumping to her feet caused a swift blow to the side of her head. Reeling from the impact,, she fell back onto the chair, and the striped tie encircled her neck. Westerkamp tightened the noose while whispering in her ear. Wendy clawed at the tie, trying to relieve the pressure, another blow to her head made her ears ring and she was on the verge of losing consciousness. When Westerkamp realized she was subdued, he released some pressure on her neck and began to taunt her, "do you want to beg Wendy, I love to hear women beg. I could tell you were ready to crack, it would be just a matter of time before you spilled your guts. You would have blamed my son; I can't let that happen". He increased the pressure once again and continued the taunting, "You're a tease, Derek told me all about your rejections, no one, especially a tramp like you from a jerk water town is good enough to reject my son. You were a virgin, you're not the first virgin I have had so don't think you are special, I wish I had more time, I would like another round with you, but conscious this time, to hear you beg," The garlic smell became stronger, the tie noose became tighter, Wendy's last thoughts were of her father, she had always wanted his love, she wondered if he would realize he loved her when she was dead, her world went dark.

Darkness was Westerkamp's friend; he knew he would be able to dispose of Wendy's body before anyone realized she was missing. He went to the janitor's closet and got a large paint tarp, he put Wendy's coat, hat, and gloves on her, placed her on the edge of the tarp with her books and rolled the body in a bundle. He dragged the bundle down the hall to the rear exit, letting her body thump down each granite step, remembering the beating his son had taken on her behalf. He threw her body in the trunk of his car, freezing rain was beginning to fall, he drove slowly through town, not wanting to cause any suspicion. When Westerkamp thought he was far enough from town, he stopped his car in a remote part of the McKinny farm. Westerkamp got the tarp out of the trunk, flipped the end, sending Wendy's body, along with her books down a steep embankment, he smiled, knowing the body wouldn't be seen from the road.

5:15 pm Boston.

The flight from Logan International to O'Hare was two hours and forty-eight minutes, Buzz relaxed after takeoff and started to review the Nelson Personnel file he acquired from the prep school. William Nelson, AKA William Westerkamp, was never in the military, his status was 4F, his wife wasn't born in Spain, she was a first generation American born in San Antonia, Texas, their son was born as Steven Nelson in Boston, and Massachusetts in nineteen sixty. To fit the Westerkamp family profile, Steven had to pose as an eighteen-year-old entering the senior class, the reality was, the kid had just turned twenty. Nelson didn't have any teaching credentials but had learned to speak fluent Spanish which allowed him the knowledge to teach the class. Buzz was going to first drop the bombshell information to the members of the school board, one member being his father. The end of William Nelson AKA William Westerkamp's position as principal, was in sight, they would be forced out of the house the school district provided rent-free as a perk, and hopefully, the family would be forced to leave Coatesville, just as they had to leave Boston, in disgrace. Buzz smiled at the prospect, the trip to Boston and being away from his family was worth the effort. Riding Coatesville of the Westerkamp family provided a hopeful outcome, little did Buzz know the information he had obtained would be too little too late for Wendy.

6:30 CST O'Hare International.

As Buzz entered the long tubular tunnel connecting the plane to the terminal, he could hear the heavy Chicago winds swirling around the circular structure. The baggage conveyor was loaded, the old suitcase Buzz had was easy to spot, he grabbed the bag and headed to the nearest departure board to check his commuter flight time, Buzz had one hour and forty minutes before departure at eight-ten. An unused phone was hard to find, Buzz went to the airport café, with a large cup of hot steaming coffee, he positioned himself in view for the next available phone.

Buzz couldn't wait to hear the sweet soothing voice of his wife, but when he finally made a connection to his home at seven o'clock, Betsy's voice was panic-stricken, "Wendy is missing." Betsy was on the verge of hysteria as she relayed all the information she had, "she never got home from school, she not at Carol's, Dennis, Jack, and Tom are searching every road for her, freezing rain has begun to fall here, Oh Buzz where can she be?" A helpless feeling swept over Buzz, he was still one hundred fifty miles from home, he said a silent prayer that Wendy would be found alive, and that his commuter flight wouldn't be delayed because of bad weather.

It was just starting to sleet when the small plane landed in Wayne County, Buzz grabbed his bag and hit the ground running; the old Blazer was colder than the Arctic when he slid his big frame in the driver's seat. Buzz hoped to be in his office by midnight, but the roads were slick, any speed over forty miles per hour caused the Blazer to slide. Buzz's two-way radio didn't have the distance to reach his office in Coates County, so he patched through to Center County sheriff's office. Red Weller was a perfect fit for a sheriff's job, he had never been married, but word had it he was involved with Honee, and that would explain how she was able to operate her 'Gentleman's club' without any hassle from the law. It was a relief to hear

Red's voice, "Hey good buddy, I understand you have a problem in Coats, Dennis called me." Buzz hesitated before responding, he didn't want to go into a lot of detail on a two-way radio, Red pick-up on the pause, "I may need some help with a search." "Anything you need, we can be in Coates in fifteen minutes, keep me posted, 10-4." Buzz signed off, "Thanks, 10-4. "

The drive seemed endless; Buzz had to concentrate on the roads, but his mind wanted to explore every possible explanation for Wendy's sudden disappearance. There wasn't one scenario Buzz could think of that would have a happy ending.

Wednesday November 6th, 1980

12:04 am.

The sheriff's office was ablaze with lights and activity when Buzz arrived, Tom, Jack, and Dennis had returned from their search to get warm and compare notes, Betty Whitfield and Carol were seated against the wall. Betty looked at Buzz with red swollen eyes, her expression matched his feeling. There probably wouldn't be a good ending to Wendy's disappearance.

Everyone was trying to talk at once, Carol was filled with grief, and her voice cracked, "Buzz we have looked everywhere, it's like she has disappeared into thin air, please, please, find her." Buzz had to restore some sort of order to the chaos taking place, he held up his hand in a 'stop' motion, silence fell among the worried group.

Buzz was thinking fast, he issued orders, "The foul weather and darkness will hinder any off-road searching, Jack and Tom return at dawn, take Carol home and try to get some sleep. Dennis, take Mrs. Whitfield home", it gulled Buzz that the Rev. couldn't have accompanied his wife to the sheriff's office to help find their only daughter. Betty Whitfield was a broken-hearted mother with no support, Buzz gently helped her to her feet, she was completely exhausted and teetering on the verge of collapse, "believe me, I want to find Wendy, I'll keep you informed, but you need to rest." Buzz and Betty locked eyes for an instant, they both knew the odds of finding Wendy unharmed decreased with each passing hour.

When Dennis returned to the office, Buzz fired up the old Blazer and headed for a drive-by the Nelson, AKA Westerkamp residence, freezing rain was pounding the windshield, driving was treacherous. Both cars were in the driveway, and the house was dark, it was a comfort knowing where father and son were, there was enough evidence to expose Nelson's fraudulent identity, but was he also responsible for Wendy's disappearance, Buzz wanted to keep close tabs on activity of the family.

Slipping in the rear entrance of his home, Buzz found Betsy dozing on the sofa. She became wide awake when he lightly kissed her cheek. The information Buzz had on the Westerkamp family caused a gasp from his wife, she had more questions than he had answers for. Betsy had some information to share with her husband, school was cancelled because of the weather, which was good news for Buzz, the principal and family would probably remain at home.

Buzz desperately missed his children, he went to the boys' bedroom to find Drake and Dillion asleep, as he approached Amy's room, he heard crying. Buzz tapped on the door and stepped inside; Amy was sitting up with her back resting on the headboard while clutching her favourite stuffed llama. Fatherly instinct made him sit down on the edge of the bed and pull her small body to his chest. Amy's words sent a stab right through Buzz's heart, "Dad, please promise me you'll find Wendy, she's the nicest, sweetest person I know." Buzz wouldn't make promises he wasn't sure he could keep, "I'm going to do everything in my power to find her, now I want you to get some sleep, your mother will need help with your brothers, I'll be home as soon as possible." Buzz tucked his daughter under her covers just as he had done when she was a little girl. As Buzz left his daughter's bedroom, he remembered how often he had promised his wife and family he would be home 'as soon as possible'. Before he reached his office he made a silent vow to his family: once Wendy's disappearance was solved, he would resign his position as the sheriff.

Dennis looked weary, Buzz sent him to the backroom to grab some shuteye before the search resumed at dawn. The time allowed him to examine all the facts, the night seemed endless. There were a few things Buzz was almost certain of, Wendy wasn't spending time with a boyfriend or an older lover, he was equally sure she hadn't run off, although with a father like the Rev., he wouldn't have blamed her. The abduction angle by a stranger was against Buzz's better judgement, Wendy would have been snatched in broad daylight in view of a lot of people she was known to. The things Buzz had learned about the Nelson family's quick departure from Boston because of an incident involving an underage girl and Derek Westerkamp, AKA Steven Nelson, made him a plausible suspect in Wendy's case. There were never any charges filed against Steven Nelson, which led Buzz to believe the sex with the girl was consensual, leaving Steven Nelson in the clear. The question lingered, why did the family depart in such a rush, or why William Nelson wanted to assume a new identity of William Westerkamp?

A whole pot of coffee later, dawn was breaking, Tom and Jack were back in the office looking like hell, but ready to move, Buzz devised a plan: the searchers were to start at the school and fan out in different directions. Buzz stayed behind to make a few phone calls, his first contacted Brant Miller asking him to check the lake areas, Brant was shocked to learn of Wendy's disappearance and was quick to offer all the help that was needed. There wasn't any fear Buzz would be disturbing Carol, she didn't sleep all night and very much wanted to be part of the search, Buzz asked her if Wendy had any personal belongings at the salon, if so to check for notes or anything that might explain her state of mind prior to her disappearance. Carol assured Buzz she would check everything, including her spare money and journal Wendy had stashed in the salon office.

7:30 am.

Carol's salon:

The weather caused all the regular appointments at the salon to be cancelled, the plants Wendy so lovingly attended seemed to know something was amiss, Carol rushed to the office, the extra money and the journal were in the bottom drawer of the filing cabinet. Under different circumstances, Carol would never invade the privacy of Wendy's personal belongings, the spare money was still in a bank bag, and the total was more than five hundred dollars. The hope Wendy was still alive diminished with the discovery of the extra cash, if she wanted to disappear voluntarily, she would have surely taken the money. Carol turned to the journal of Wendy, she was shocked by the number of entries pertaining to winning her father's love and approval, only to be rebuffed over and over by the Rev. There were entries about the word "Winter", and the cost of fifty dollars as a debt, it didn't surprise Carol at all, she knew about the brothel and the girls who used the four seasons for their working names. The big surprise came to Carol when she read about Wendy's suspicions about the possibility that the Rev. was the peeping tom. Carol's hatred for the Rev. Leroy Whitfield only intensified, she knew she now had damming information on good Rev., enough to at least ruin his reputation in town and maybe to have the Rev. ousted from the ministry altogether. Carol read of the good times Wendy had spent in the company of the people who did love her, tears filled Carol's eyes when she read of the love Wendy had for her. Reading each entry very slowly, Carol started to grasp the loneliness Wendy endured but tried to make the most of her life every day. Wendy made mention of her feelings changing for Calvin Anderson and questioning her decision about opting for a closer college. The next entry stunned Carol,

"On Monday, October 27th, I was raped by Derek Westerkamp in the supply closet at school. The lights went out, I couldn't see anything, Derek came up behind me with his strong Boston drawl and hissed in my ear, 'You caused the beating', he was blaming me for his assault. He knocked me over the head, I must have passed out, when I regained consciousness, I realised I had been raped, and I sensed something else, the strong smell of Garlic. I thought it was my imagination, but the odour lingered in the closed closet, overpowering the usual smell of banana oil. I can't stand the smell of garlic anymore, I am frantic awaiting my period, I pray I'm not pregnant. My deepest fear is my father finding out about the rape, he must never know, he will blame me for being a wanton woman that he talks about in his sermons. I would become a disgrace to him, a damaged daughter and labelled a whore. There isn't a single person I can confide in; every avenue would lead straight to my father. I feel so alone and ashamed."

After reading the entry, Carol was gasping for breath, horror, panic, and anger filled every fibre of her soul, she had to get in touch with Buzz.

8:30 Sheriff's office.

Buzz was ready to set out in the search efforts, Jack and Tom checked in, they had checked the IGA area, the Ruritan grounds and were ready to search the bridge and stream banks, they realised the search probably wasn't a rescue effort anymore but a body recovery effort. Dennis was moving in the direction of the Anderson Farm; Buzz was going to head toward the McKinny farm. The freezing rain was subsiding, but the wind was bitter, just as Buzz turned on the Old Post Road, he saw Luis Santos, one of the regular farm hands on the McKinny farm, with his collie dog running, waving his arms for Buzz's attention. Luis slid alongside Buzz's Blazer, grabbing the side mirror to keep from falling on the icy road, a look of fright was on the farm hand's face, his English was mixed with Spanish, from what Buzz could understand, he and his dog were searching for Wendy on a remote area of the farm, Luis and the dog jumped in the blazed and headed to the location. Buzz brought his Blazer to a halt, Luis showed him what the dog had sensed, from the top of the embankment, Buzz could see what appeared to be a body lodged halfway down the hill. Buzz knew what he was looking at, it made him sick, the slope was steep, he had to sidestep down the hill, but there wasn't any doubt it was the body of Wendy Whitfield. The lifeless body was covered with a thin coat of ice, Buzz looked at the blueish skin of a once loving and vibrant girl, he hit the ground on his knees. Buzz hadn't cried in a very long time since his days in Vietnam as he looked at the faces of the small innocent children and saw the horror, they faced every day. Now he looked down at the body of a young girl who never hurt anyone, she had the capacity to love and not be critical of a person's shortcomings. She had helped Amy with her pre-algebra, Wendy was the one who was wise enough to see the good qualities of people and not listen to a lot of gossip. Buzz suddenly realised Wendy's parents would have to be informed, and Carol, who was probably closer to Wendy than any other living soul.

Buzz was unaware of the rain falling or the bitter wind sweeping the hillside, he wanted to pull Wendy to his chest just as he had done with his daughter just a few short hours ago, but the lifeless body could no longer accept or return the love she was once so willing to share. The overwhelming feeling of grief had Buzz looking toward heaven asking, "Why", he brushed the ice from Wendy's face, and there on her neck were what appeared to be ligature marks. Buzz's anger coursed through his body, upon closer examination, he saw defensive wounds in the form of fingernail marks on her neck above the ligature mark around Wendy's neck, which meant she had fought for her life. Buzz agonised over Wendy's last moments alive, the panic and terror she must have endured at the hands of a murderer, his adrenaline started to pump, anger and revenge. As Sheriff Buzz knew he had a job to do, making his way back up the hill, he grabbed a roll of yellow crime tape from the Blazer and started back down the embankment, after securing the scene he called Dennis on the two-way radio. Dennis was in the sheriff's office when he answered Buzz's transmission, the news was devastating, Buzz ordered his deputy to call the county coroner and advise him of the location of the body. Dennis told Buzz, "Carol has called twice and needed to speak to you as soon as possible," Buzz dreaded breaking the news of Wendy's murder to Carol, but it was part of his job.

By the time the county coroner arrived, Jack and Tom were at the scene, they had heard the news on the two-way radio, and Dennis had the task of visiting the Whitfield's home to break the news of Wendy's death. Jack and Tom looked on helplessly as Buzz and the coroner went down the steep embankment to view the body. Wendy's body was fully clothed: panties, bra, nylons, shoes, shirt, blouse, winter coat, knitted hat and gloves, which led Buzz to believe that no sexual assault occurred, so what was the motive? The coroner viewed the marks on Wendy's neck, his preliminary assessment was death by ligature strangulation, which is what Buzz thought. There isn't much evidence in what is considered 'a soft kill' in police investigations: no bullet wounds, no stab wounds, and usually no hair or fibres. Robbery was ruled out, Wendy's purse contained a good deal of cash, along with her student ID, the books found were standard issue textbooks, which led Buzz to believe she was either murdered at school or soon after. An autopsy would be performed for the final cause and estimated time of death, but regardless of the results, Buzz was investigating the murder of a beautiful young girl.

Buzz was glad the weather was bad; the streets of Coatesville were almost deserted as the hearse carried Wendy's body through town. Tom and Jack accompanied Buzz to break the news to Carol, when she saw the expression on their faces, she collapsed. Tom gently pulled Carol to her feet and held her close as her deep wrenching sobs turned to whimper. Buzz and Jack stood by, feeling her pain. Time stood still, finally, Carol regained her composure, handing Buzz Wendy's journal and telling him to read the entry of Oct. 27th.

Buzz began to read, the word Rape jumped off the page, it could be a motive for murder, Wendy named Derek Westerkamp as her rapist, he blamed her for the assault that had taken place, and the rape was revenge. The whole picture changed when Buzz read the line about the strong smell of garlic. Buzz stored every bit of info in his mind no matter how insignificant it seemed when interviewing the girls at Honee's house, he remembered Autumn told him 'Nelson' as he referred to himself when visiting the brothel, reeked of garlic when he became sexually excited. Both William and Derek had the same Boston drawl, Wendy blamed Derek, Buzz knew differently. When Buzz finished reading, he paused a minute, planning his next move, Carol was impatient, "Is that enough proof to arrest Derek for rape and possible murder ?" "No" was Buzz's reply, which enraged Carol, she lunged at Buzz,

"Why ?" Buzz looked at the trio, waiting to hear his reasoning, his answer shocked them, "It wasn't Derek that raped and possibly murdered Wendy, it was William Westerkamp. I will need to take the journal for evidence, I will need you to verify the writing as Wendy's, I will return the journal to you once this matter has been resolved."

5:15 pm.

Darkness had fallen by the time Buzz left the salon, he shared Carol's pain, but she had the support of a loving husband and father. Buzz wondered how Betty Whitfield reacted to the news of Wendy's death; unlike Carol, Betty didn't have any emotional support, the only source of love she ever had was in the back of a hearse on the way to the morgue.

Dennis was completely spent when Buzz arrived back at the office, apparently, the meeting with the Whitfield family hadn't gone well, after the initial shock of the news, Betty Whitfield never spoke a word, she sat on the sofa staring, not looking at anything or seeing anything. Buzz gave the journal to Dennis, "Read the October 27th entry, then I want you to set up surveillance at the Westerkamp residences, no one is to leave the house. I've got to call Betsy to check in with her, and Judge Krebs to prepare a search warrant. Red Weller's department will be helping with the search." Dennis's anger matched Buzz's when he finished reading the entry in the journal and understood Buzz's orders. Everyone was dog-tired, but no one wanted Nelson, AKA Westerkamp, to escape prosecution.

It seemed like ages since Buzz had spoken to his wife, Betsy knew from Buzz's tone the news wasn't good, but she was horrified to hear the details of the rape and murder. Buzz hated placing the responsibility on his wife, acting as a single parent once again, but it was important to get justice for Wendy and Betsy agreed. Buzz reminded Betsy how much he loved her and ended the conversation like he ended so many calls to his wife, "I'll be home as soon as possible."

Judge Krebs was a very grim-looking man with jowls that drooped like an old hound dog, he had a pinched nose and wore a pair of wire-rimmed glassed. Buzz referred to the Judge as Judge Crabs. The judge was all about the due process, he had a lot of heated discussions with Buzz about the law. Buzz argued, that laws and justice were two different things, it seemed in due process, the suspect had more rights than the victim. Due Process allowed a lot of grey areas and loopholes in the laws, Buzz saw the law as right and wrong. The phone rang four times before the judge answered, Buzz didn't have time for a lot of formalities, "Judge Krebs, this is Sheriff O'Neil, I need a search and seizure warrant for the residence of William Nelson, AKA William Westerkamp at six Old Post Road. I also need an arrest warrant for Rape and suspicion of First-Degree Murder for William Nelson, AKA William Westerkamp. There was a brief pause, Buzz expected a lecture, but instead, the judge asked to repeat the names and addresses and said the warrants would be ready in an hour.

Judge Krebs lived in Union, close to the northern border of the county line, the round trip would take about two hours with the weather conditions. Dennis radioed the office from his surveillance position; everything was quiet at the Westerkamp residence, Buzz was on his way to Union, he couldn't remember the last time he slept in his own bed, the last rest he had was the cheap motel in Boston with the ugly green wallpaper. Buzz was able to make better time than first anticipated; the rain had stopped, and the roads were drying off. Judge Krebs was waiting, the front porch light came on when Buzz pulled into the driveway. The judge had the warrants in his hand when he opened the door, but he wanted to speak to Buzz before relinquishing the documents. Judge Krebs never minced words, "Let me give you a nickel's worth of judicial advice, if you want this guy, make sure your T's are crossed and your I's are dotted, no discrepancies in the paperwork." In a fatherly gesture, the judge placed his hand on Buzz's shoulder, "I know the bonds in a small town, if this is personal for you, which I think it is, No Brutality with the suspect, make sure you read the Miranda rights to this guy verbatim, we don't want a smart defence attorney to have anything to hang their hat on."

10:15 pm.

Red Weller, Buzz, and three deputies descended on the home of William Westerkamp, AKA William Nelson, Buzz pounded on the front door until he heard footfall and an angry voice, "Who is it?" William Westerkamp was incensed by the late-night intrusion; Buzz shoved the search warrant at him and pushed around Westerkamp while the other four men followed. Mrs Westerkamp and Derek were standing on the stairs, startled and puzzled by the police activity, William demanded to know the reason for the raid. The outburst unruffled Buzz, "Read the warrant, I want the family to remain in the living room while the search is done. Where are the keys to the two vehicles parked in the driveway?" Derek was stunned; Mrs Westerkamp was compliant, she fetched the two sets of keys and took a seat next to her son on the sofa, which lead Buzz to believe she had lived through this same scenario more than one time. The two Center County deputies went outside to process the two Westerkamp's vehicles, Dennis started in the lower level of the residence, Buzz headed upstairs. The master bedroom was Buzz's focus, the closet had a full-length mirror on the outside, and on the inside of the door was a wooden shelf with pegs holding dozens of ties, a perfect weapon in a ligature strangulation. A long metal pole extended the width of the closet crammed full of clothing, all men's apparel, with no shortage of shoes, hats and overcoats.

Wendy had deep lacerations on her neck, the weapon might possibly have blood stains, Buzz examined each tie. There was a total of twenty-six ties, and none of the ties had any evidence of blood or hairs, Buzz turned his attention to the shoes, looking for mud. The shoes and ties proved to be a dead end; Buzz was starting to question his theory. Buzz took each suit out of the closet, hung each piece on a peg and looked in every pocket, his heart skipped a beat, a grey suit had the faint odour of garlic. The grey jacket's inside pocket contained a red and white striped tie rolled up into a ball. Buzz found three small rusty brown stains, he was sure this was the murder weapon and that a lab would find the stains to be blood, consistent with Wendy's blood type. The suit and tie were marked as possible evidence, a Center County deputy appeared in the doorway and announced he had made a discovery in the trunk of Westerkamp's car. The discovery turned out to be a large canvas tarp, the combined evidence was tagged and bagged for the lab.

Red Weller stood guard in the living room; Westerkamp was shouting obscenities and accusations at the Center County sheriff, everything from invasion of privacy to unlawful police procedure. Red got his nickname because of his ruddy complexion, which brightened when he was angry, at that moment, his face was scarlet in colour. Buzz entered the living room, "William Nelson, AKA William Westerkamp, I'm placing you under arrest for rape and suspicion of the murder of Wendy Whitfield." The smug expression on Westerkamp's face disappeared, Buzz was eager to put the handcuffs on Westerkamp's wrists. The words of advice Judge Krebs gave Buzz echoed in his mind by the book, the Miranda Rights were read slowly and deliberately, "Do you understand these rights ?"

Mrs. Westerkamp looked at her husband with total disgust, her attitude told Buzz a lot about the family's past and their sudden departure from Boston. Buzz felt a twinge of pity for Derek Westerkamp, AKA Steven Nelson, his father had the whole family living a lie, assuming fraudulent identities to protect his father's past indiscretions, only to have history repeat itself.

Thursday November 7th, 1980

Coates County Sheriff's Office.

No one would ever know the amount of hatred Buzz had for the man sitting in the holding cell awaiting the arrival of the state police to take Custody of Nelson. On several occasions,

Nelson would taunt Buzz with snide remarks about the 'Mayberry Jail', the thought of kicking Nelson's ass while alone at the office crossed Buzz's mind, but the Judge's words echoed again, "by the book, NO Brutality."

It was after six o'clock on Thursday morning before Buzz was able to leave the sheriff's office and get home to his family. After so many days with no sleep and the tenseness of the situation, coffee didn't even do the trick, Buzz slept for fifteen hours. No one bothered Buzz in those fifteen hours, when he finally awoke all the horror came flooding back to him. William Westerkamp, AKA William Nelson, was in the hands of the state police and the district attorney, Buzz wondered if Coatesville would ever be able to recover. Wendy's funeral would be a horrific reminder of the evil that had invaded Coates County in 1980

Tuesday November 12th, 1980

Wendy's autopsy arrived early on Tuesday morning at the sheriff's office, Buzz made all sorts of excuses for not reading the report, there were the end-of-the-year reports to be filed and the proposal for the prospected sheriff's budget for nineteen eighty-one to be approved by Coates County, that had to be completed. Buzz couldn't concentrate on the new year with the old year looming large and the funeral for Wendy to be held on Thursday.

The people of Coatesville were less apprehensive after the arrest of Nelson, AKA Westerkamp, but the arrest left the school district without a principal. Nelson was looking at the rape of a minor, and premeditated first-degree murder, which carried a life sentence without the possibility of parole or the death penalty.

The autopsy report was standard issue with all the seals and signatures of the Pathologist, it seemed so cold and unyielding with all the proper medical terms one expects of such a report, but unaware of the beautiful young girl whose life was cut tragically short. The cause of death was listed as ligature strangulation with the hyoid bone crushed, Buzz took no pride or pleasure on being right about the method of death. The death was ruled a homicide, after reading the report, Buzz agonised over the last few moments of Wendy's life, the terror and panic she must have endured at the hands of Nelson, it was at that moment, Buzz hoped the jury would opt for the death penalty.

Buzz was sure Derek Westerkamp, AKA Steven Nelson, was responsible for the vandalism on the McKinny Farm and the robbery of the small general store owned by Mac and Dolly, but he didn't think the kid robbed the IGA or had a part in Wendy's death. The only thing Mrs. Westerkamp, AKA Mrs. Nelson, was guilty of was assuming a false identity, she never spoke a word or offered any kind of assurance to her husband as Buzz practically dragged Nelson from the family's residence the day of his arrest.

The Coates County school board held an emergency meeting to decide the fate of the two remaining members of the Westerkamp family regarding the home the family occupied belonging to the school district. The board opted to let the two remaining members of the Westerkamp AKA Nelson family stay in the residence until other arrangements could be made, Buzz had the job of delivering the notice. Mrs. Westerkamp opened the door, Buzz found both Derek, AKA Steven and his mother to be remorseful and completely devastated over the rape and murder of Wendy. When Buzz departed from home, he thought William Westerkamp probably didn't have any support from his family or a friend in the world, a very smart lawyer would be his only hope.

10:00 am.

Relief from total exhaustion and mental anguish had come in the form of a sedative prescribed by Dr. Bender for Carol, she slept for sixteen hours. Upon waking, she was disoriented, sunlight was coming through the bedroom window, Carol didn't know what time it was or even the day of the week. The past came flooding back in vivid detail. Wendy was murdered, and suddenly, the time or day didn't matter. Carol got out of bed and sat at her vanity, the bright sunlight was unkind to the mirror image she was staring at; her hair was tangled and needed to be washed, and her bright green eyes seemed dull and lifeless. Carol opened the vanity drawer and pulled out a snub-nosed revolver, it felt cold and cruel in her hands as she stared down at the gun, turning it over and examining the foreign object, but it would provide an end to her pain and suffering. Carol looked at her image, she saw her father standing in the doorway, it took Jack Furry three giant strides to be at his daughter's side, he pulled her from the settee, held her arm's length and shook her like a rag doll, "do you think Wendy would want to be the cause of another senseless tragedy ?" Suddenly Carol's mind cleared, she dropped the gun on the floor and fell into her father's arms and sobbed like a small child, "Why didn't I see the stress Wendy must have been under, why her, she never harmed anyone, what could I have done to prevent her death?" Jack gently pushed Carol away to look at her face, "I don't have the answers you need; I know I'm supposed to be full of fatherly advice and answers, but it is tragic experience I've never dealt with, I lost you once due to my gambling addiction, I can't bear the thought of losing you again. Your brother has arrived, he is downstairs, Tom is worried sick about you, I want you to shower, dress and come to the kitchen for something to eat."

Some people might think Jack's action with his daughter was cruel and heartless, but to Carol, it was a check of reality. The Permanent Solution Salon was closed for business since the death of Wendy, the shop was a constant reminder of the young girl who brought so much joy to everyone's life. Carol unlocked the door and stepped inside the salon. Everywhere she looked were signs of Wendy, the plants she had so lovingly named and taken care of seemed to be drooping. The supply room was a testimony of Wendy's organisational skills, and every shelf was labelled and stocked neatly, and a pile of fresh laundered towels and capes were stacked on the dryer.

Carol went to the salon office. The ledge book's neat listings of debts, credits, and balances, all written in Wendy's handwriting lying on the desk, seemed like business as usual, but things would never be the same. There was a small wall safe in the office. Carol dialled the three numbers, listening for the tumblers to click, inside was a seventeen-year-old secret. Carol retrieved a ten by twelve inch while envelope, yellowed by age, that contained two documents. The documents were birth certificates for a set of twins, Carol's twins, which she had lost. Carol smoothed her fingers over the tiny footprints, listed as the mother was Carol Ann Furry and listed as the father was Clark Lee Taylor. Carol's mind drifted back seventeen years:

Carol's mother was right, the once ugly duckling turned into a beautiful swan during her junior year. Miraculous changes started to happen, Carol became the spitting image of her mother, just like she had promised. Carol developed a full, shapely figure, perfect almond-shaped green eyes, gorgeous mahogany hair, and a beautiful, even skin tone. The girl who was once the subject of ridicule and humiliation by her classmates, instigated by Clark Taylor, was now the centre of attention. The changes in Carol didn't go unnoticed, Clark Taylor wasn't any exception, so it wasn't surprising when Carol received a phone call from the superego Clark requesting a date. Carol despised Clark, she had suffered years of constant torment because of him, she graciously accepted his invitation for a date, when she hung up the phone, a smile played on her lips, she was ready to exact her revenge on Clark Taylor. The plan was simple, Carol wanted Clark to believe he had won her affection, she would feed his oversized ego, when she would destroy him in front of all their classmates and toss him aside like trash. The plan was working out, one date led to another. Clark confessed he was head over heels in love with her, but there was a hitch in Carol's plan, she was falling in love with Clark, she wanted to give him everything, including her virginity. She dreamed of a wedding after he completed college and settling down in a cosy home while Clark practised law, the starry eye dreams of a life with him came to an end when

Carol discovered she was pregnant. The news of a pregnancy outraged Clark, he kicked her in the stomach and told her to get rid of the bastard kid. Once again, he was able to destroy Carol, her plan had a devastating ending. Clark screamed at Carol, he was going to be a senator and couldn't explain a tramp wife like her, whose mother was a waitress and a father who had abandoned the family. Carol's revenge had backfired and left her pregnant.

Clark's father, Dr. Roy Taylor, was equally as nasty about Carol's untimely pregnancy, he stormed into Carol's home uninvited and demanded she have an abortion. Ruby Furry, Carol's mother, was infuriated by the intrusions and rejected the idea of an abortion, she also reminded the doctor his son played a role in the pregnancy. A plan was devised: Carol would spend her entire pregnancy at Lakewood Sanitarium, she could continue her studies, the baby would be delivered at the Lakewood General Hospital and given up for adoption. Dr. Roy Taylor was willing to pay all the expenses to cover his son's indiscretions, no one questioned Carol's sudden disappearance or the story of helping a dying relative with the children in another state.

It was a surprise when, on May 25th, Carol delivered twin girls under very heavy sedation, Carol did regain consciousness long enough to see the two tiny bundles lying in clear plastic cribs and to sign the necessary adoption papers. Carol reserved the right to name her baby, but with the birth of twins, she had to change her choice.

Carol sat at her desk and wept, she looked at the birth certificates and wondered what might have been, she read the names out loud: Mandy Lynn died fifteen hours after birth due to complications during delivery and the other baby was named Wendy Lee. Carol planned on telling Wendy she was her birth mother when she turned eighteen, the legal age in the state, but that would never happen.

Dr. Roy Taylor contacted a young minister coming to Coatesville about adopting the surviving child, when Rev. Leroy Whitfield arrived in town with his wife, Betty, they had a newborn daughter named Wendy. Carol often wondered if the local adoption was meant as a cruel reminder to her and Clark of their indiscretion or if Dr. Taylor wanted to watch his granddaughter grow up. Dr. Taylor made Clark have a vasectomy as further punishment, but if he thought he would further punish Carol by having Wendy reside in Coatesville, he was mistaken, she was happy to see Wendy become a beautiful young lady.

Carol was lost in thought, suddenly she realised she wasn't alone, her father was standing in the doorway of the office. Jack looked at his lovely daughter, he needed to offer her some comfort, "this is a sad time for me as well. Wendy was my only grandchild." That statement caused Carol's body to jerk in surprise, "you knew ?" Jack sat down across the desk, "Carol, when I was forced to leave the family because of my gambling, your mother and I were still very much in love. She wrote to me about everything you and Mike did, good or bad, right or wrong. I knew where you spent your pregnancy, I knew about the birth of twin girls and the death of the one child. I was glad you were able to continue your studies and return to Coatesville and graduate with your class." Carol was relieved, the secret she had carried for seventeen years wasn't a secret at all, "I don't know who I hate more, Wendy's murderer or the Rev. who rejected her love for so many years. Jack's response concerned Carol, "The justice system will take care of Westerkamp, I'll take care of the Rev. Leroy Whitfield."

Thursday November 14th, 1980

Wendy's funeral.

Thursday dawned clear and sunny but cold and blustery, the wind swept the streets of Coatesville as if cleaning the evil that invaded the town. The church was packed with over two hundred people who came to pay their respects. Dozens of bouquets of flowers overflowed the altar. Wendy's casket was white, lined in pink satin, the lid was open, exposing a beautiful young lady who appeared to be sleeping peacefully while a freshly dug grave in the old cemetery waited as her final resting place.

For two days, Carol tried to find some inter-strength to face the funeral, but her emotions betrayed her as she entered the church and was confronted with the sight of Wendy's casket. The combination of stress, grief and the overpowering scent of the flowers brought Carol to the verge of collapse. Tom guided her to a pew; Carol exchanged an unspoken silent moment with Betty Whitfield. The adopted mother and birth mother shared the same heartbreak, Betty Whitfield sat alone, her shoulders were slumped, and her body looked to be deflated of life. Carol felt a sense of pity for more than herself.

Betty, Calvin and Clifford Anderson selected the six pallbearers, were Wendy's closest male classmates, and Buzz O'Neil was the likely choice, but it was surprising that Jack Furry was chosen, Jack and the Rev. were on less than friendly terms. Carol's husband, Tom and her brother, Mike, rounded out the group, each man sat solemnly in the front row but deemed it an honour to be chosen for the task.

Evonne accompanied by Robert Newman, sat with Carol along with Nan, Dolly and Mac. Amy O'Neil persuaded her parents to attend the funeral. She sat with her mother, Betsy, and the Miller family, Ty, Brant, Sueme, and Bill. The Rev. Adam Wedgewood, the head of the church council, would be delivering the eulogy; his wife Ann and Gus Johnson sat with Betty Whitfield. It didn't escape anyone's attention that the Rev. Leroy Whitfield was absent from his wife's side while bustling through the crowd of mourners, making small talk as if it was a regular Sunday Service.

Mummers filled the air when Clark Taylor entered the church; many folks blamed Clark for his recommendation of

William Westerkamp for principal, and others disapproved of the brassy blonde sharing his residence and his abuse involving Evonne. Clark Taylor was well dressed, sober, and without the blonde, he resembled the Clark everyone knew in past times. Evonne held her breath, wondering if Clark would make a scene. Instead, he seemed totally unaware of her presence, he walked straight to the casket and said something inaudible to the crowd as if he was talking to Wendy. No one was more surprised than Carol when Clark stopped at her pew and offered his most sincere condolences, "I'm sorry Carol, for everything" he never looked at his ex-wife and left the church quietly. Carol was almost sure the quiet conversation at the casket was expressing remorse for never acknowledging Wendy as his daughter or sharing any part of her life, no one would ever know for sure but Clark.

Missy Evans, Wendy's best friend, walked to the front of the church. Twenty-two members of the senior class at Coates County School passed by Wendy's casket and handed Missy a yellow rose, she bound the flowers with a yellow ribbon and placed the bouquet next to Wendy's body.

The school choir sang Amazing Grace and The Old Rugged Cross while the two hundred mourners passed by the casket for their final farewell. No one knew the internal strength Carol had as she looked one last time at the still-lifeless body of her precious daughter.

Rev. Adam Wedgewood seemed like a kind and sincere man, but it pained Carol that he had only met Wendy on one occasion. He wouldn't be able to speak honestly of her kindness and generosity or her boundless love and compassion. Rev. Adam spoke of the grieving process, the cruel reality and the untimely death of Wendy, "we expect to bury our elderly parents, but nothing can prepare us to bury a child." The church was silent except for sobbing and occasional wailing of grief, even the strongest men had tears flowing, none more so than the Anderson twins.

The eulogy concluded with the hymn 'Shall We Gather at The River', which the congregation sang in unison. The mourners were asked to leave the church while the funeral director and crew closed and sealed Wendy's casket. Carol sat frozen, unable to move; she couldn't endure the thought of the casket containing Wendy's body hovering over an open grave as the Rev. said a final prayer. Carol felt a gentle nudge on her arm, it was Evonne and Nan by her side, the time had come to face reality: Wendy was gone, the casket was forever sealed, and the cold, hard earth awaited.

The funeral was over, there wasn't anything left but to go home and allow the grieving process to begin. Dozens of bouquets were carried from the church by the funeral crew, awaiting the departure of mourners to close the grave. The crowd was dispersing, seeking shelter from the relentless wind, Tom and Mike had completed their task as pallbearers and gathered with Carol and Nan, but Jack wasn't anywhere to be found.

The church was eerily silent, Jack waited patiently in the office, he didn't disrespect the house of worship, but the Rev. Leroy Whitfield defiled this house for years. Jack lit a cigar and blew slow, lazy circles of smoke toward the ceiling, the preacher's bible was lying on the desk, Jack opened the book and turned to Numbers, Chapter 32:23, "Be sure that your sin will find you out." Jack found the dark clothing Wendy saw her father wearing, suspecting him of being the 'peeping tom', and was stacked neatly beside the open Bible on the preacher's desk. When the Rev. appeared in the doorway, he stopped in his tracks at the sight of Jack casually smoking in his office, his eyes dropped to the desk and saw the clothes and Bible. Jack's voice was dangerously low, "Close the door, Rev.." The Rev's voice bellowed throughout the office as he grabbed the dark clothing, "Get Out, Furry", this isn't the time or place for more of your threats. The desk chair almost tilted over as the Rev. threw his body in the seat, he stuffed the dark clothing in a drawer and slammed the Bible closed. Jack didn't flinch, "No your wrong, it's a perfect time for a chat, you see I just spent the majority of the day here in church to bury my granddaughter because of you." Rev. Leroy's face was red, twisted with anger, he lunged across the desk at Jack, "You're blaming me for Wendy's death ?" Jack's voice was a dangerously low whisper, "did you know Wendy kept a journal? Do you know how many times her entries involved seeking your love and approval only to have her love rebuffed by you. Do you know she was raped at school by the same man that murdered her and carried that torment because she didn't want to tarnish your reputation? She couldn't tell a soul of the horror she endured for fear you would consider her damaged and label her a whore. If she could have revealed the rape, we may not have had to bury her today. I warned you before, so you have two choices: you can leave town quietly or I'll expose your sins to the church council which you hold yourself in such high regard. I really think they'll take a dim view of your 'peeping tom' activity and using church funds for paying prostitutes. You have until Wednesday, when the council meets again to make your decision. Either way, you're finished." Jack took his half-finished cigar and stubbed it out on the desk blotter and strolled out of the church office, leaving the Rev. Leroy Whitfield to decide his own fate.

Friday November 28th, 1980

In the two weeks since Wendy's funeral, the people of Coatesville were forced to move on, Ronald Lawyer, the sixth-grade teacher at Coates County School, was named temporary principal. The Anderson twins, Calvin and Clifford returned to school just as Lester Anderson said would happen when William Westerkamp was gone. The diner was operating on a regular schedule, but the conversation and gossip was a little more subdued. Carol reopened the Permanent Solution, she decided to open only three days a week, the loss of Wendy was still hard to deal with; the Blackjack Trucking Company was serving the area farmers and businesses. Gus Johnson refused to print the story of the tragic murder of Wendy in the Coates County paper, he said the event would be forever a part of history in the county, but the story would never appear in print.

There were some changes in the county. Residences were more apprehensive with strangers; while doors and windows were locked, it would take a long time to overcome the evil that prevailed in the fall of nineteen eighty.

4:00 pm. Sheriff's office.

Buzz was serving his last full day as Sheriff of Coates County; it was a shock to the community when his resignation was filed in the county courthouse. Deputy Sheriff Dennis Miller would be sworn in as acting sheriff until a special election could be held, but it was almost certain Dennis would be voted into office.

Buzz had been thinking for months about resigning, he had been drafted at the age of eighteen, the US government placed a gun in his hands before he was allowed to vote. He served his military time with honour but never wanted to see the death and destruction of another war. The sheriff's position was appealing when Buzz was discharged from the Marine Corps, he had a desire to provide safety and peace to his community, but Wendy's death proved him wrong. Buzz didn't blame himself for the death, if he had known about the rape, the murder might have been prevented. Buzz felt he had paid his dues, sometimes at his family time expense, Betsy had held the family together long enough.

Buzz had hoped to solve the IGA robbery, but he left all his notes and photos on Dennis's desk, he had no doubts about the deputy's ability and no regrets about his decision. The final act of his term as sheriff was removing his badge and service revolver and locking them in the office safe.

Betsy was thrilled by the career change. Taking over the feed and grain mill meant regular hours, no postponed meals, and no phone calls in the middle of the night, waking up the whole family. The office phone rang, it was Betsy reminding Buzz her parents were coming for supper. His usual response was, "I'll be home as soon as possible", but today, he was able to tell his loving wife, "I'm on my way home."

M L Pensinger

EPILOGUE

Saturday August 23rd, 1983

The small town of Coatesville recovered slowly after the tragic events in the fall of nineteen eighty. Wendy Whitfield's murder would have a profound effect on the residents for a long time. Wendy's senior class erected a statue of an angel with spread wings as if ascending to heaven, the plaque read, "Wendy an angel on earth", which was placed on the grass cul-de-sac in front of the high school. The Coates County school board awarded Wendy a diploma posthumously, the five hundred dollars Wendy had saved was given to the school library in her name.

William Westerkamp AKA William Nelson, was tried and convicted of first-degree murder and given a life sentence without parole plus fifty years for rape, the death penalty was taken off the table in return for Nelson admitting in open court to the rape of Wendy. The two remaining members of the family left town soon after William Westerkamp AKA William Nelson's arrest. Derek Westerkamp AKA Steven Nelson and his mother were never charged with any crime. Their whereabouts are unknown.

On May twenty-fifth, nineteen eighty-one, the date of what would have been Wendy's eighteenth birthday, Clark Taylor committed suicide, his conspicuous consumption of material possessions and drinking had taken its toll, he died a drunken, penniless, broken man. The date of Clark's untimely death didn't escape Carol's attention, his cruelty and passion for causing misery to others had come home to roost.

The Rev. Leroy Whitfield was stripped of his ministry after curtain facts relating to the church funds were brought to the attention of Adam Wedgewood, the head of the church council. Pleas for mercy fell on dead ears, and information provided by Jack Furry against the Rev. was overwhelming. The church ledger proved the preacher was bilking money with fraudulent fund-raising schemes while using church funds to pay for his lavish lifestyle and the sexual entertainment he sought at a local brothel. The preacher didn't have the capacity to love others, only himself. He held everyone else in contempt. From the pulpit, he spewed hatred for women and sexual misconduct when he was guilty of perverted sexual perversion. With the fraud, sexual improprieties and hypocrisy exposed, the Rev. Leroy Whitfield was forced to leave town, no one in town knew or cared where he disappeared to.

Betty Whitfield remained in Coatesville, she divorced her husband soon after his quick departure, she had finally rid herself of the loveless marriage. Betty was able to provide information proving her husband was the 'peeping tom', she followed him one night and found the good preacher peeping in Nan's windows. Carol and Betty shared a common bond, Wendy, the birth mother and adopted mother made peace with each other's love and loss. Carol cut and styled Betty's hair and helped her adapt to a modern and stylish wardrobe, the changes brought to light Betty's intelligence and self-confidence. Betty began to get involved with civic affairs and became a major influence in preserving the history of Coates County. No one was aware of the bachelor's degree Betty held in education, she was always forced to stand behind her husband and under his thumb. The degree proved advantageous to the county; Betty became the first female principal of the Coates County school district. Betty purchased the foreclosed home of Clark Taylor for pennies on the dollar and restored the house to its former glory.

Gus Johnson sold the Coates County Courier; he remained a member of the Coates County school board but was ready to do a little fishing in his retirement. Ty McKinny sold Gus the cabin on the lake. He was like a grandfather to Buzz's children and was a frequent guest in the O'Neil home.

Dolly and Mac closed the general store, their generosity hadn't diminished with age, the remaining inventory was donated to the local food bank. Dolly was suffering from the first stages of Alzheimer's disease, Mac was plagued with arthritis, the couple who had contributed so much to the community needed help, the residents of Coatesville responded. The townspeople provided transportation for doctor's visits, helped with daily chores and marketing, and everyone became involved in the preservation of the historical general store, ensuring it didn't fall into a state of disrepair.

Todd and Susan Baker had become a well-adjusted, happily married couple. With the help of Evonne, Susan studied for and obtained her GED, she was promoted to manager of the cafeteria in the school district. Todd kept his word to Jack Furry about his terms of employment, he stopped drinking and was an asset to the Blackjack Trucking Company. Randy Baker was excelling in school, winning the state-wide spelling contest, he gave his blue ribbon to his favorite teacher, Mrs Evonne Taylor. For so long Randy felt like an outcast, unable to keep up with the other students until one teacher came along and realised he didn't have a learning problem just a vision problem.

Buzz's resignation saddened the residents of Coates County, but they understood his desire to devote more time to his family and relieve Betsy's responsibility of being a single parent on many occasions. Shorty after Buzz's departure from the sheriff's office, his love for his wife became apparent when Betsy discovered she was pregnant. It looked funny to see big strapping Buzz carrying a little pink bundle, they named the new addition to the O'Neil family, Wendy Lee.

Nan was able to quit the diner after twenty-nine years of service when she married Jack Furry with Carol and Mike's complete blessing. The couple moved to the new house on the trucking company's property. Nan flourished in her new life, she was able to pursue her passion for gardening and cooking, while Jack enjoyed the company of a loving wife and eating home cooking. The Blackjack Trucking company was a success from the start, the county's farms and businesses increased their net profit with the lesser cost of local delivery charges, while Jack posted substantial earnings.

Mike Furry had experienced a costly relationship with Carm while still in the military, he wasn't in a hurry to settle down and test the waters of matrimony. Cross country trucking suited Mike, it provided a sense of freedom being on the open road. He bought Nan's house, he knew one day he would have a wife and family, but Mike was going to be more cautious in selecting a lifetime mate.

Carol and Tom's three-year marriage was everything she had hoped for, Tom was running his rig locally and home every night, and the Permanent Solution salon was busy, but Carol cut her hours to three days a week. The couple took frequent weekend trips to enjoy the outdoors and each other, the decision was made not to adopt a child. Carol's recovery time from Wendy's death was slow and painful, she wouldn't be able to bare burying another child if something unforeseen happened.

Rev. Ronald Blessing replaced Leroy Whitfield as the pastor. By all accounts the new preacher lived up to his name, a blessing to the town. The old church took on a new life, the outdated building with a dank odour and sermons of hell, fire, and damnation was transformed. The congregation rallied around Rev. Blessing; a fresh coat of paint was applied to the chipped yellow walls, the threadbare carpet was replaced, and the bare windows were covered with brightly coloured drapes. The church's membership increased as did the tithing, as a result of the messages preached by Rev. Blessing. The flim-flam artistry of bilking money from the hard-working parishioners ended, as well as the intimidating sermons. The church became the sight of many happy events. On August twenty-third, Evonne Shultz Taylor and Robert Newman were married with the Rev. Blessing presiding.

3:00 pm. The McKinny Farm.

Evonne and Robert's reception was in full swing; the bride and groom arrived at Robert's Harley after the wedding. The celebration had a bittersweet flavor; Evonne and Robert would be leaving the area and moving to the deep northwest. The decision Evonne made was an easy one, she loved her friends, but it was time to go home and assume the responsibility of the massive family tree farm and her aging parents. Robert was fully on board with the move, it seemed ironic Evonne met the man of her dreams because of an abusive, failed marriage. Evonne accomplished her dream of teaching, she was able to change the life of one student profoundly, Randy Baker, she would never forget the young boy. The bride and groom were beaming as Gus snapped pictures, preserving the event as a part of Coates County history.

It was time to cut the cake, Ty hurried to the house to see if the final preparations were complete. Ty observed the happy couple mixing with their guests. Evonne's departure from Coatesville saddened Ty, but she more than most understood the importance of family. In the middle of the crowd was her loving husband, Brant, with their three-year-old son riding high on his shoulders. Ty scanned the crowd for Sueme, in the three years since her arrival, she had become an American citizen and more importantly a member of the McKinny family.

Sueme's sixteenth birthday was approaching, she mastered the sport of riding with blue ribbons of her own, she was tri-lingual and spoke better English than most Americans. Ty remembered the envelope that was delivered long ago addressed to her, from the Department of the Army. Ty knew it was the final report on the government's investigation into the parentage of Sueme that she had demanded. Ty pulled the envelope off the shelf, turning it over in her hands, it was still sealed, no matter the contents; Sueme was her daughter, and nothing would ever change. Ty struck a match to the envelope and watched as the flames licked the edge, then tossed it in the fireplace. Ty thought of all the ghosts attending the party, including Sonny her brother, who had suffered a tragic farming accident when she was just nine years old. Her mother, Pauline who never recovered from Sonny's death. Her father, Samuel, whose death brought Brant into her life, and her ancestor, Harrison McKinny, who gave up everything in his homeland, enduring tremendous hardships to come to America, providing her with the life she had come to cherish. Suddenly, the baby Ty expected around Christmas kicked, reminding her that life was for the living, she put the past in its place, walked out into the sunshine and joined the celebration.

The End

Acknowledgment

My special thanks to my son-in-law, Eddie, for his technical support.

A special thanks to my pen pal in New York, Ilean, for proofreading and undying support through the process.